When Diego Champagne realizes that he can't live without Colby Young, he comes up with a plan that will free him from the Banni motorcycle gang forever. He's prepared to leave everything behind and make a new life for the man he loves and the children for whom Colby is now responsible. But he can tell no one, not even Colby if he hopes to carry it off.

Colby's having problems accepting that if he's to remain the guardian of his niece and nephew, he must stay clear of the Banni, and that means Diego. Given Colby's past, he's being watched like a hawk, and not just by Child Protection Services. Then Colby's world spirals out of control when a member of the Banni informs Colby that they found Diego's body burnt beyond recognition, along with his vest and bike. Miserable and angry at the world, Colby ends up in more trouble, his entire world held together by a thread.

Meanwhile, Diego must fulfill a promise to the leader of the Texas Crushers, who ironically helps him escape from the Banni life. Putting miles and time between him and the man he loves, Diego sets the wheels in motion that will prepare the stage for a crime-free life with Colby and the children. Question is, how will he tell Colby he's not dead, and will Colby ever forgive him for keeping the truth from him?

CONTENT ADVISORY: This is a re-edited, re-release title.

Permanent Moonlight
Copyright © 2019 A. J. Llewellyn and D. J. Manly
ISBN: 978-1-4874-2507-4
Cover art by Martine Jardin

Published by eXtasy Books Inc or
Devine Destinies, an imprint of eXtasy Books Inc

Look for us online at:
www.eXtasybooks.com or www.devinedestinies.com

Permanent Moonlight
Rough Riders Book 4

By

A. J. Llewellyn and D. J. Manly

DEDICATION

Burn rubber, not your soul, baby.
— Craig Fernandez, Biker Boyz

TRADEMARKS ACKNOWLEDGEMENT

The author acknowledges the trademarked status and trademark owners of the following wordmarks mentioned in this work of fiction:

.357 Magnum: Smith & Wesson Corp
Accurate Engineering Outlaw: Accurate Engineering
Autumn Leaves: music by Joseph Kosma; lyrics by Jacques Prevért / Johnny Mercer
Baker: Baker, Inc.
Be Nice to Spiders (1967): written by Margaret Bloy Graham
Being Dead Is No Excuse: The Official Southern Ladies Guide to Hosting the Perfect Funeral: written by Gayden Metcalfe and Charlotte Hays
Britten: Britten Motorcycle Company Ltd.
Coke: The Coca-Cola Company
Corvette: General Motors LLC
Dat Dog: Dat Dog Enterprises, LLC
Delta Air Lines: Delta Air Lines, Inc.
Ford: Ford Motor Company
Google: Google Inc.
Harley-Davidson: H-D U.S.A, LLC
Hotmail: Microsoft Corporation
Jack Daniel's: Jack Daniel's Properties, Inc.
McDonald's / Mickey D's: McDonald's Corporation
Mixmaster: Sunbeam Products, Inc.
Mr. Deeds Goes to Town: Columbia Pictures

New Orleans Music Exchange: 3342 Magazine Street, New Orleans, LA

Nu Hotel: Nu Hotel Toronto Inc.

People Magazine: Time Inc.

Realtor: National Association of Realtors Corporation

The First 48: A&E Television Networks

Toyota: Toyota Jidosha Kabushiki Kaisha TA /aka Toyota Motor Corporation

Valium: Roche Products Inc.

Viagra: Pfizer Inc.

CHAPTER ONE

Colby

It rained the day we buried my sister, Garnet Beauty. I mean, really buried her. Not hurling her off into some forest in a weighted-down cooler. I saw it as a good omen because they say that if you've never ridden your motorcycle in the rain, you haven't ridden at all.

I had my sister cremated and took her ashes for a ride around town, one last time, so she could feel the breeze before I let her go forever. I had her urn strapped to the seat behind me, my tears freezing midway down my cheeks.

She was the best riding companion a guy could have.

I was surprised how many people came to the little ceremony I had at the Windy Hills Memorial Park. So many friends I never knew came to listen to the minister, who'd definitely never known her, make kind comments about how Garnet was Heaven's Beauty now. Yes. I believed she was in Heaven. I tried not to think about how I'd last seen her. Skeletal remains in a science lab. So many people had cared and, I could see, still did. Many wept, and I realized her life may have been short, but her story was still being told. Saying goodbye was not the ending I wanted, but it did make me feel better that countless people I had never met had been touched by her life and untimely death.

"When I think of Garnet Beauty," the minister said, "I am reminded of the words, 'Let your children be as so many flowers, borrowed from God. If the flowers die or wither, thank God for a summer loan of them.'"

Shit. He put tears in my eyes.

And then Rogan Duchesne, the cop who'd been my sole support system and the man who'd hunted down my sister's earthly remains, and those who killed her, moved forward and spoke.

"I'd like to read a poem," he said. "It's called 'Young Life Cut Short,' its author, however, is unknown." He cleared his throat.

> *"Do not judge a song by its duration*
> *Nor by the number of its notes*
> *Judge it by the richness of its contents*
> *Sometimes those unfinished are among the most poignant . . .*
>
> *Do not judge a song by its duration*
> *Nor by the number of its notes*
> *Judge it by the way it touches and lifts the soul*
> *Sometimes those unfinished are among the most beautiful . . .*
>
> *And when something has enriched your life*
> *And when its melody lingers on in your heart.*
> *Is it unfinished?*
> *Or is it endless?"*

Man, oh man. There wasn't a dry eye left, in spite of the rain having stopped. The minister took over as Duchesne rejoined the line of cops slightly to the back of our huge group. I recognized a few of them as the men from Alabama who'd first discovered my sister's abandoned, abused body, and after being unable to identify her, paid for a grave for her out of their own pockets.

I hoped wherever she was flying, my little girl could see that people did care. We loved her. I loved her. After the minister spoke and prayers had been said, I turned on a boom-box I'd brought with Eva Cassidy singing 'Autumn Leaves.'

It's the song I most identify with Garnet Beauty. As Eva's clear, resonant voice sang, I emptied Garnet's urn into a shallow hole in the ground. On top of this, I planted a peach tree. She was a young 'un, like my sister, and of course, she was a Garnet Beauty. I couldn't bear the idea of Garnet alone in a wooden box or in an urn forever. She'd been kept in a cage in life, but she was free now, part of the earth, part of a tree.

"Goodbye, astral angel," I said when the song ended. I patted the damp, fragrant earth, and ashes around the root of the tree. I really lost it then. My brothers-in-arms from the Banni were all there. They'd all brought flowers. Some brought fruit. Strangers brought teddy bears and dolls. For the first time in three weeks, I felt Diego's arms go around me, and I trembled, both from his touch and the nearness of him.

I watched people leaving things around the tree. I didn't want her here. I wanted her home, happy, laughing, and running free. She was still a thing of beauty though, and she would always hurt my heart. Wherever I went, she would always be with me. My best friend Jerry hugged me. His mom, Sue-Ellen, wrapped me in her arms. "She's in God's hands now, darling," she said. And I knew she was reminding me that no human hand would ever touch my little sister again.

Missing from the service that sad, gloomy Saturday, were my father, who was on a jailhouse hospital respirator, and his lover and criminal accomplice, Calvin, also presently incarcerated. And so was my sister, June Gold. All three had been involved in the death and coverup of my sister's gruesome murder.

Also missing was my crazy mother, Evangeline, who'd

been in a nuthouse for years. Last time I saw her, she was holding a headless doll in her arms. Apparently, she still does. She spanks it and calls it Colby. And, oh yes, my sister's husband, Judd, wasn't there. He, too, was in the big house on unrelated murder charges.

When I chose the minister for the service, I'd picked the one who seemed the least judgmental. He made no claims to know God's thoughts, like the minister I spoke to before him who tried to tell me, "God will never kill you. He will squeeze you, but never kill you."

I thought that was very inappropriate considering we were burying my murdered sister.

This minister though, Calhoun was his name, was cool. He had a soft spot for kids, and motorcycles it seemed. I had spotted one in his backyard when I went to his house. He said, "The death of a child is the hardest goodbye there is in this world."

Yup. He had that right.

I suppose that's another reason so many people showed up the day we buried Garnet Beauty. Small and innocent, she'd been in and out of the newspapers the last dozen or so years. And there was the curiosity factor. I'm the guy who's had so much crap happen to him. I sometimes wonder how the hell God expects a person to endure so much. On top of it, I wanted to be the legal guardian of my niece and nephew, Garnet Beauty, named for my sister, and little Henry.

To do that, I'd had to quit the Banni. And Diego. But I hadn't quit him. Not really. We still spoke, and I still spent time with his mom, Cherise, but the kids were a big part of my world. I'd had to enlist Sue-Ellen's and Jerry's help. She's the official foster mom, and we all live in New Orleans now, in a big crumbly, historic house, and I've taken over June Gold's bakery.

What I know about baking you could squeeze into a

thimble, but I'm learning fast. Welda Stonestreet, our DCFS, dropped in frequently and asked the kids questions. She had been known to open the fridge and check for food. She even checked the laundry hamper to make sure we were keeping their clothes clean.

The children weren't at the service either because I don't believe that funerals or cages belong in a kid's life. Cherise was at home recuperating from chemo, looking after the kids. Henry has been fussy recently. He was close to my sister, his mother, and cried for her. Little Garnet, however, had blossomed. My sister was mean to her, so that's no surprise. But I could feel the tug of the kids' hearts calling me. I wanted to get back to them. I needed to see them and love them, to shadow all my pain.

I swiveled my gaze toward Diego, who looked like he might be missing me, too, and then a woman who might have been beautiful once approached me.

"I'm Anjohnette O'Reilly," she said in a tone that suggested I should know who she was. I looked her up and down, trying not to be too obvious. She looked a little long in the tooth to be a reporter, but then again, what the hell did I know? I glanced up at her hair and should have known when I saw how pale and blonde she was. I should have seen the family resemblance.

"I'm your mom's half-sister," she said.

I just stared at her.

"Your grandpa, your maternal grandpa, had a whole other family. I don't suppose June Gold ever told you about me."

Nope, she never had. And I stared at this woman wondering how it was that June Gold knew about her and I didn't. I tried to do a little rough family history in my mind and realized my grandpa had never divorced, as far as I knew. Which meant he was a cheater. Man, I came from a long line of dickheads, didn't I?

"When Evangeline had the two girls, I got to know them some," Anjohnette said. "I offered to take them many times." A bitter note crept into her tone and a strange gleam swept across her pale blue eyes that made me think of Evangeline, and the comparisons weren't flattering. I hated Evangeline for ruining our family and keeping my sister in a cage.

"I've given June Gold a lot of money over the years," Anjohnette went on. I almost laughed.

"So have I."

She nodded. "I suspected as much. The DCFS tells me you have the two wee ones in your care, but June called me from prison and said she wanted me to take custody of the children."

The words fell over me like a musty, wet blanket. I started to sway. I'd done everything the Department of Children and Family Services of Louisiana, or DCFS had required. I had been going to family therapy sessions three times a week in four-hour blocks to learn how to parent. They had actually been very cool, teaching me how to talk to the kids about their wayward parents and why they weren't around. I had completed two intense weeks, with two more to go. I'd proved my bank accounts were healthy and that I could afford to raise the kids in the manner in which they'd become accustomed.

Our caseworker dropped in frequently to check on us all. I'd done everything the state demanded and would continue to do so.

"I have no intention of taking those babies from you," Anjohnette said. "But you are all the only family I have." Her gaze fell to the ground. "When my husband Silas died three years ago and my funds dried up, so did my access to the children. I used to babysit Garnet Beauty often, but I have never even met little Henry."

It didn't surprise me that June had chewed up and spat out the poor woman, but it did surprise me that she'd never mentioned her. I felt compelled to invite her to the wake.

"Oh, Sue-Ellen already extended an invitation," she said.

Anjohnette looked spookily like my mother except that she seemed rational. Still, their reed-slim builds, long blonde hair and faraway beauty were so alike, it gave me pause. I didn't think I could ever get close to her. I'd chat to my caseworker, Welda Stonestreet before I let Anjohnette loose on the kids.

"See you there," I said. I wondered how many other people would show up to the home I'd just purchased on Coliseum Street to raise my new little family. It was a five bedroom, three-and-a-half bathroom house that had been built in what realtors liked to call the shotgun style but had been extensively refurbished as a camelback home, complete with a swing set and vegetable garden in back.

Jumping on my motorbike, I sped to the house, worried that we wouldn't have enough food.

I arrived seconds before half the city did but needn't have worried. I should have known with all the Southern belles in my life that we'd have plenty of food and drink. As I walked across the blond hardwood floors, I fell in love with the place all over again. Its location was a godsend considering the bakery was in the heart of the French Quarter. Everything was white inside, right down to the marbled bathroom floors and their double sinks.

The smell of fresh paint was still strong, and I inhaled deeply. Ah. Cornbread. I followed my nose into the kitchen where I discovered a frazzled-looking Cherise unloading huge pans of hot chicken salad casserole, a Southern specialty, out of the oven. My mouth began to water at the array of dishes. Southern fried chicken with cornbread dressing;

Shipwreck Casserole, which was comprised of beef, potato, and other vegetables; and shrimp gumbo.

She had made three different kinds of iced sweet teas, also known as the champagne of the South, and punch, pasta dishes, rice platters adorned with barbecued pulled pork, and other tasty meats. And oh, man, the desserts. I drooled over my favorite, Watergate Salad, made up of fruit salad, pistachio pudding, and marshmallows and extra pineapple.

I was startled to see a cookbook on the kitchen counter entitled *Being Dead Is No Excuse: The Official Southern Ladies Guide to Hosting the Perfect Funeral.*

"Be a lamb," she said, "and take these into the living room."

I did as she requested and found that the human vultures were already helping themselves. Rogan Duchesne sidled up to me, a beer in one hand, and a hot hunk of cornbread in the other.

"What do you think of Nuts?" he asked me out of the corner of his mouth.

"Nuts?" It took me a moment to register whether he meant the food variety or the absolutely crazy biker dude who got his nickname from the copious amount of nuts that he ate. I saw the lustful look exchanged between them.

Oh, brother. "You know he's um, well, nuts, right?" I asked, an instantly regretted it when I felt Duchesne bristling beside me.

"Maybe," he said, pressing his lips to my ear. "But he gives damned good head."

He moved away, and I stood, slack-jawed, a moment and watched him walk over to Nuts. I already knew things were difficult for Duchesne. He'd obsessed over my sister's disappearance for so long, he had nothing else, no other cases that consumed his passion. He had his own missing sister, and he sort of knew what happened to her, but he had no body and therefore no physical proof of what her killer had confessed to.

And he had no chance for a funeral.

I watched him take a nut out of his apparent lover's ever-present bag and grabbed a Watergate Salad that had been served in a cut-crystal goblet. It looked to be the last one left. As Nuts and Duchesne chatted animatedly, I looked away, trying not to think of the two of them having sex. I'd never known whether Duchesne was gay or not. I'd suspected he was, because, frankly, he was so damned nice, but discovering that Nuts was, came as a huge surprise. It hit me in all the wrong ways because Diego and I had been forced to meet in secret and to stay away from one another because being gay was a death sentence in motorbike gangs.

People came past me offering condolences as I ate. I appreciated their kind words, but I was distracted. Somebody was staring at me, and from the way my body was reacting to the scrutiny, I knew it was Diego. When I finally spotted him across the crowded room, his face creased into a smile. I wanted so badly to slip away with him, but first, I had to locate my kids.

"Where are Garnet and Henry?" I asked Cherise who swept past me with a laden platter of steaming crawfish.

"They're with the Calhouns." She beamed at me. "Such a nice family. They just came by and picked them up. We thought it was better that they shouldn't be here when everyone came from the funeral."

I wished she'd consulted me, but I liked the preacher and his kin. I nodded, spooned the last delicious mouthful of creamy fruit salad into my mouth and swapped dishes with her. I took the platter out of her hands and kissed her forehead. I was so happy that the minister who'd conducted the service was as nice as I'd thought he was. He and his wife had two kids around Henry's age, which was three. A little young for Garnet, but she loved children of all ages. She was a little mother, that one.

Cherise's skin felt warm to my lips. "You didn't overdo it, did you?" I asked, anxiously. She had opted for two months of chemo, to be followed by a three-month regimen of a different drug to treat her ovarian cancer. She had managed to keep her hair thanks to a cold cap remedy she used during her chemo sessions. What she couldn't control was crushing tiredness and a tendency to flush crimson for a few days after the sessions.

These were balanced only a little by hydration and white blood cell therapy sessions the day after chemo. She had four weeks to go, and her doctors had said they were pleased with her progress. They had assured us that the second phase of treatments would be easier than the first.

"I feel great," she said. "I wish I'd discovered edibles sooner!"

Edibles. Oh, geez. I glanced around, fearful that Welda Stonestreet might have overheard. All I needed was for that pesky DCFS caseworker to know that Cherise was a pothead. Well, technically speaking, she was a truffle head. The edibles I purchased for her were expensive chocolates with marijuana blended into them. The pot was undetectable unless they were left in a warm room. They helped her, and she helped me, so I was happy to foot the bill for her treats.

"We need to pick the kids up by four. Garnet has her ballet class at four thirty." Cherise blew a kiss over to her son, who mimed catching it. It was now noon, and I had plenty of time to collect the little ones, but I was a man with a mission, and I zeroed in on Diego, who must have read my expression correctly. He inclined his head, and after I deposited the crawfish on the already full table, I migrated toward the back door.

I spotted Welda Stonestreet chatting with Sue-Ellen. I

caught her stuffing a chocolate into her mouth and panicked, hoping it wasn't an edible.

"The kids are doing great," I overheard Sue-Ellen saying. "I honestly think they get a lot more attention these days. June Gold used to keep them at the bakery night and day."

That was true. I'd seen the children really open up and laugh more now that the adults caring for them insisted that they have a childhood. I felt a momentary pang of grief wondering how my sister had gone so wrong.

Money. That's what it was. I've always believed in the value of hard work, and I suppose I'm lucky in that I invested in businesses where other people worked for me. My sister was obsessed with cash, and I'd helped her often through the years, but it was never enough. She always wanted more, more, more.

Outside in the backyard, I watched my neighbor's bunny hop on over to the purple carrots the kids, and I had been carefully tending. I'd never hated a creature more in my life. Henry would be devastated that his favorite vegetables would be gone.

"Excuse me," I told Diego who was waiting for me by the swing set. I picked up the bunny just as it started chomping at the leafy, green carrot tops. "Can you sneak away?" I asked him, straightening again.

"I can. Can you?"

"Sure. I'll meet you at the motel. Give me ten minutes."

He opened and closed his mouth. His bleak expression said it all. I experienced deep, personal satisfaction that he was missing me, too, and I marched over to the neighbors to return their wayward rabbit.

A few minutes later, I slipped around the side of their house and set out for Diego's motel on foot. It looked like he had, too, because I noticed his brand-new Harley-Davidson still parked out front.

One of the things I loved about the house was its close proximity to trendy shops and restaurants on Magazine and Prytania Streets. I'd chosen the motel for Diego and booked him into it.

When I arrived at his second-floor room, he opened the door before I could even knock.

"Get in here," he said, pulling me toward him. It was my favorite kind of greeting. Our mouths met as he shoved the door closed with his foot.

Hungry for each other, we devoured with lips and tongues, hands frantically beginning the strip search I'd longed for each and every day.

Naked, our cocks collided, and we naturally reached for one another.

"Fuck," he said against my mouth. "I could never give you up." He kissed me harder and deeper and suddenly began to laugh.

"What's funny?" I rasped, anxious to get my mouth on his cock.

"Welda Stonestreet."

I almost got an iffy stiffy. "Say . . . what?"

He nodded, stifling the laughter that didn't seem appropriate when we had so little time. "She asked me what kind of girls you go for. She says you're too sexy to be single and celibate."

"What did you tell her?"

He put his hand to my cheek, cupping it for a moment before moving it down my chin and over my throat. He reached my chest, bit his lip, and pushed me to the bed. "I told her you weren't my type, but I supposed some might call you sexy."

I fell to the bed with a soft thud, and he crawled over my body. I needed the skin-on-skin contact.

"The things we do for love," he whispered as his mouth

bore down on mine again.

I accepted his kisses but had other things in mind. I pushed him off me, satisfied by his impassioned, "Hey!" Pushing him onto the bed, I rolled him onto his back.

"You got any body oil or lotion handy?" I asked him.

He touched his rigid cock and looked up at me. "Baby oil," he said. "My skin's been dry lately."

"Where is it?"

He jutted his head toward the bathroom, and I got off the bed, my own hard cock bouncing like a buoy in the breeze. I found a black bag on the sink and opened it, surprised to find a fistful of condoms in it. I picked up a few. What the fuck? Since when did he cart around rubbers? We'd stopped using them. Had he been anticipating finding someone new? Was he fooling around?

I dropped them back in the bag and took out the baby oil. I had to remind myself we'd sort of agreed to stay away from one another . . . but that didn't mean we'd be seeing other people.

Did it?

I tried hard to keep my anxiety and mounting anger in check. I would raise the topic later. Right now, I had a man to pleasure. And, damn him, I'd make sure he didn't forget this afternoon any time soon. I returned to the bed and found him lying there playing lightly with himself.

"You ever experienced the torpedo, Diego?"

He looked up at me, frowning. His hand stopped moving. "The torpedo? No, I don't think so. What is it?"

I knelt on the bed beside him and brushed his hand away from his balls. "I'm going to make you come over and over again, without touching your cock."

He raised a brow at me. "You don't want to touch my cock?"

"No," I snapped.

"Don't you miss it?" He gripped it and shook it toward me. I melted because he was just so goofy and endearing right now.

"No."

"No?" A beat. "Something wrong, Colby?" He started to get up, and I pushed him back down again.

"The condoms."

He rolled his eyes. "That's just for show. I packed in front of the others."

I knew he was telling me the truth and felt stupid for acting like a girl. "I'm sick of hiding." I kissed his chest. "I'm sick of shadows."

"Me, too, babe." He wriggled under me. "So, what's the torpedo?"

I was about to ruin everything. I needed him to be calm and happy in order for it to work, but I just couldn't stop myself. "Why do we have to hide when Nuts and Duchesne are openly lusting after each other?"

"What?" He exploded with laughter. "What are you talking about? You been eating my mom's edibles?"

"Nope." I uncapped the baby oil.

"Oh, geez. I'm sorry to disappoint you, but there's no romance going on there. Nuts is trying to sell him a high-end motorbike. And maybe invest in his new nut shop."

Nut shop? That was news to me. With a pang, I realized I'd missed out on so much being here in New Orleans with the family. "Really?" I kept my tone light. "Then why did Duchesne tell me Nuts gives such good head?"

Diego looked stunned. A look of uncertainty crossed his face. "Oh, man. I don't think even Nuts would blow a guy for the sake of a few bucks."

I shrugged and squeezed the oil into my hands. I warmed it and placed my palms on his chest. He grinned up at me.

"You promised to make me come hard. More than once.

Without touching my cock. Was that an idle threat?"

"No. It was a promise. Mind you, I've never tried it before."

He looked uneasy now. "What's involved, exactly?"

"Your pure and total pleasure."

He opened and closed his mouth. Then, "Wait. If you've never tried it, how do you know about it?"

"My sister's sex videos."

He screwed up his nose. "Eew! Your sister made sex videos and you watched them?"

"No, dufus." I playfully smacked his head. "She bought them. They're all educational ones. Tantric sex videos. I watched 'em all and stashed them in my office safe at the pool hall. DCFS will never know about them."

He smiled at me then, the delight in the promise of sexual gratification returning to his eyes. "And it's called the torpedo?"

"Uh-huh. You ready?"

He nodded eagerly.

"Close your eyes."

"Why?"

"Because you're supposed to relax, and I need to concentrate."

He stared at me.

"Close them!" I barked, and he dutifully obeyed. If only he was always so compliant.

I took a deep breath and moved up on the bed so that I was behind his head. I rubbed more oil onto my hands, placing them on his shoulders and pushing them gently down. It was supposed to start the relaxation process. I felt the shift immediately.

Damn, this thing works! I began rolling my palms and the back of my hands against his shoulders, inching forward and down his torso. I backed up and pressed my now very warm palms into his pecs and waited a few seconds. I moved down to his nipples and began massaging them. I kept moving down toward his crotch, then coming back up. By now I was focusing on the body meridians the video had described, and I could almost see the lines running down his body. Each time I crossed from one imaginary line to another, he bucked under my touch.

He kept moaning as I worked, and I knew he was feeling very good. Within a few minutes, his back arched and his cock grew very hard. He moved his hand down, and I yelled, "Don't!"

Diego grinned but kept his eyes closed.

For several long minutes, I focused on his chest, nipples, and then his belly. His whole body almost flew off the bed. I moved back up and started on his pecs again. I checked the time on the clock radio beside his bed. I knew I had to build up the sexual tension in order for him to have his greatest release. Ten minutes flew by, then fifteen, then twenty.

He began to sweat and thrash on the bed to every touch. I eased off touching him. The longer this took, the harder his orgasm. I began working on him again. His cock started to leak. Man, this thing worked fast. I moved farther down his body, then back up again. This went on for another twenty minutes, and his impassioned moans could probably be heard for miles. He didn't know what to do with himself.

His head tossed back and forth, his skin reacting to every stroke of my fingers.

It was time.

I got up on my knees, leaned over his body and pressed all five fingers of my left hand right into his solar plexus. He shot so hard, come spewed everywhere. He came with a roar, his body twisting and turning. I removed my hand. I still didn't touch him. Ten seconds later I pressed my fingers into him again, and he came even harder.

16

"Fuck!" he screamed. "Fuuucck!"

I kept working him slowly. Wherever I pressed my fingers, his body reacted. He came five times and tears streamed down his face. It didn't matter where I touched him; he came hard five times in a row. He lay back spent, his skin drenched.

"Don't touch me," he moaned. "I can't take anymore."

"That my friend, was the torpedo."

"Holy fuck. I want you to do that to me every night. You have to teach me how to do it. I want you to come like that. I never—" His words fell away, and next thing I heard was his deep, rumbling snore.

"That's the way I like my men. Rode hard and put away wet," I said, saluting him. I wanted to clean up but was afraid if I touched him with a wet towel his body would start sparking another orgasm.

I waited several minutes, and then my cell phone rang. I checked the readout, experiencing a moment of severe guilt. "Hi, Cherise."

"Don't *hi* me, young man. Where's my son?"

"I . . . er . . ."

"Listen. I know you've run off for a nooner. I've been covering your ass for the last hour."

No, you haven't. Your son has. Not that I said this aloud of course.

"Welda Stonestreet's been asking about you. She wants to see the kids. I told her you and Diego went out for ice cream. Don't make me out to be a liar, Colby. Go pick me up at least four containers. Go to the Creole Creamery. Make sure one of them is maple oatmeal. That's her favorite." Her voice dropped. "And hurry. We're just about all out of food."

We ended the call, and I glanced at Diego, who still hadn't moved a muscle on the bed. He opened his eyes finally and looked at me, a dazed expression on his face.

"You okay?" I asked, knowing he wasn't.

"Fuck, no. I'm still coming. How'd you do that?" He passed a hand across his eyes. Heh, heh, heh. He wouldn't be straying any time in a hurry. I was certain of that. "I gotta take a shower." He raised himself on one elbow, and I leaned in for a kiss. "Don't touch me!' He backed away from me. "You and your lethal hands."

He got off the bed and walked away on shaky legs.

I was almost sorry I hadn't touched his cock now. Almost. It had been worth every second of seeing him go berserk the way he had. And to think that was just one move I'd learned.

He showered quickly, and we both got dressed.

"I feel bad you didn't have any fun," he said, kissing me at last.

"Oh, I had plenty of fun." I grinned at him.

"One day, we'll have no borders," he said. We traded glances that spoke volumes.

"Let's go," I said.

We went down the back way but didn't run into anybody we knew. We walked to Prytania Street and hit the ice cream bar. We tried samples and picked out five different kinds, including the maple oatmeal for Welda Stonestreet. We'd also picked out lavender and honey ice cream, salted caramel, and unusual but tasty blue cheese and walnut ice cream, with a couple of sorbet blends for good measure.

As we walked back to my house, he said, "I've been thinking about what you told me. I'm a little worried, Colby. I can't believe Nuts would suck Duchesne's cock just to get money out of him. On the other hand, maybe Duchesne was joking."

"Maybe." I didn't think so but what the hell did I know? I shifted freezing cold cartons from one arm to the other. We'd divided the load, which helped.

18

"Yeah. You're not convinced, and neither am I." Diego really looked worried now. "Something's hinky about all this, Colby. I'm really worried now."

When we reached the house, Welda was in the front room discussing the kids with Cherise, who looked wiped out.

"We have to put the needs of the children first," Welda was saying. I tried not to react. I wanted to scream, *I've changed my whole life for those kids. We all have! All we think about are their needs!*

But I didn't.

There were still a lot of people in the house, but I couldn't immediately see Duchesne or Nuts anywhere.

Marcel, another Banni, sidled up to us. "Maple oatmeal. My favorite."

Cherise began to dole out bowls of ice cream. Welda looked the happiest I'd ever seen her. She was a large African-American woman, but she carried her weight well. She always wore color-coordinated outfits from head to toe. She had hair embellishments of every shade; shoes too, apparently. Today was black, I guessed because of the funeral service, but she still presented a vivid way about her. Perhaps it was the miniature black crib and baby set atop her spiraled hairdo.

I tried not to stare at it and handed her a bowl of ice cream. She'd devoured it before I'd even tried a bite of mine.

"I'm going to see the kids," she said. "I have three other families to visit today." She and two of her minions bustled out of the front door. I looked over my shoulder, watching her walk and wondered if she would be giving us a good or bad report.

"Wow," she's intense," Cherise said, wiggling her brows.

"Yeah." I was careful not to say more. I took a spoonful of ice cream. Delicious. I began to really miss the kids and decided to go over to the Calhouns' to bring them home.

19

"I'll walk with you," Diego said.

I nodded, pleased for his company, and his close proximity.

"Babe, I gotta thank you. I feel fucking fantastic after the torpedo. I've had a headache for days that's finally gone. And damn, I feel really good!" He grinned at me, then the smile slid a little from his gorgeous mouth. "I talked to Marcel. He says it's true. That Nuts and Duchesne are an item."

Oh, man. This was not good news. Most of the Banni, most bikers, in fact, were serious homophobes.

"I'll talk to 'em." His tone was gruff. I knew he was really nervous about how this would impact the club. And I wondered what the hell it would do to Duchesne's career. Being gay wasn't exactly an asset on the force. Not in Louisiana. We reached the Calhoun house, and as we walked through the front gate, I saw the front door was wide open.

Oh, man. More bad news. I could feel it in my bones.

I heard a dog's faint barking, and the hairs on the back of my neck stood up as we moved forward. We both stopped.

Bloody footprints on the hardwood floors leading to two stone steps and the front yard.

"Oh, God."

I'm not sure who said it, but maybe we both did. We inched forward.

"Colby, I'm taping this with my cell phone," Diego said.

"Good. Okay. Shit. The dog stopped barking."

We stood in the doorway and with the sleeve of my shirt I edged the door open a little more.

The place looked like a bloodbath.

"Oh, no." Diego's anguish mirrored my own. I looked just inside the entrance, and there was Welda Stonestreet, lying dead, shot right in the head. The two women she'd brought with her lay crumpled beside her. The barking dog, or we assumed it was the dog that had been barking, lay near the sofa. Also shot. And now very dead.

The Calhouns were also shot. Mrs. Calhoun sat slumped on the edge of the sofa and the minister lay face-down on the floor.

"Where are the kids?" I asked, my voice cracking.

We took off our shoes and walked inside.

Another man and woman were dead in the kitchen, also shot. But there was no sign of the kids. Not mine, nor the Calhouns'. And as I turned around to look at Diego who was calling 9-1-1, I saw the message in what I assumed was blood, scrawled across the living room wall: Faggots.

CHAPTER TWO

Diego

The scene in front of my eyes was flooded with cops. They seemed to swarm around me like a bunch of menacing bees. Cops made me uneasy, especially if there was an army of them. And I was really upset by all this on all kinds of levels, the murders, the word scrawled in blood, but especially the missing kids.

Colby had called his cop friend, Duchesne, and he'd come running as usual. I was pretty sure he was half in love with Colby, but I'd never tell Colby that. He'd say I was jealous. Maybe I was. I wanted to comfort him, but I kept my distance.

The cops knew who I was, and of course, they eyed me suspiciously, even though I'd taken off my vest and was holding it in my hand. One of them, a big, burly fellow with a brush cut kept looking at me as if he either wanted to fuck me or throw me in a jail cell. My money was on the latter scenario.

I should have left before the army of emergency vehicles arrived, but Colby was upset over the kids. I knew he wanted me to wait with him. As soon as I saw the cops, I got out of the way. Right now the dead wagon was carrying out bodies. Jesus. This is unreal.

Colby stood a few feet away, talking to Duchesne, who seemed at a loss for words. He kept hugging Colby, which bugged me since I'd been told he liked men, Nuts, in particular. He must have liked pistachios a lot to put up with Nuts' crazy habits. A car pulling up to the curb across the street distracted me from that thought. A man got out of a dark Plymouth. I couldn't help but notice. He was grotesquely obese and short, no more than around five-foot-five. A mop of red hair fell over his forehead, and I could see that his big round face was smattered with freckles. He wore a grey suit with a white shirt. Honestly, he looked like some kind of beached whale. He came to stand a few feet from me. He surveyed the scene for a moment then he looked over at me. He approached me as if it was some kind of a challenge, his chest puffed out. He lifted his chin as he waddled toward me.

"There you are," he announced. "What are you still doing here I wonder?"

I looked down at him. He didn't even come to my shoulder. His green eyes were shiny like a snake's. "Who might you be?"

"My name is Elmer Flint." He flashed his card. "DCFS." He didn't offer his hand. "And of course, we all know who you are."

I lifted an eyebrow. "We do?"

"They told me you were a smart mouth."

"Who are they?"

"You didn't answer my question. What would the leader of the Banni be doing here at a crime scene?"

"I'm a concerned citizen."

He laughed. "Right." He glanced at Colby. "He'll lose those children if you don't back off. Leave him alone, Diego, and let him raise those kids in a decent, God-fearing environment."

God-fearing environment? WTF. "You found the kids then?"

"We have them, yes. They were brought to DCFS an hour ago."

"By whom?"

"This isn't your concern or the concern of the Banni."

I took a step toward Colby. I intended to relieve his mind about the kids.

The DCFS guy put a hand on my forearm.

I glanced at him. "I don't recommend you touch me."

He removed his hand and took a step back. He had the good sense to look scared for a second. "The police will tell him shortly."

"What about the minister's kids?"

"Safe."

I breathed a sigh of relief.

"You really put on a good show." He brushed something imaginary off the front of his lapel. "Do you actually care about him and those kids? I mean, as much as someone the likes of you can care about anything or anyone."

"What do you think?"

"I think somewhere deep down in that tough, cool exterior, you might. So, back off." He met my gaze.

"Who in the fuck are you really?" I gritted my teeth.

"Can't you read?" He went to take out his card again.

I clenched my fist. "Yes, I can fuckin' read."

He put the card back in his pocket. "You know what I mean."

"Whose cock-sucker are you?"

He gave me a cold smile. "You'd know more about sucking cock than I would."

My jaw tightened.

"You really want to hit me right now. It's not easy holding back, is it, Diego?" He smiled. "Go ahead." He looked around. "We're surrounded by cops."

I took a breath and unclenched my fist. "Lucky break for you."

"Not a break. I know you're much smarter than that. Actually, you're the smartest leader the Banni has ever had. Too bad, you're going to wind up dead. It won't be much longer now."

"That sounds like a threat," I said, watching as a police officer walked over to talk to Colby. They were telling him the kids were all right.

Colby looked at me, utter relief on his face.

I looked away.

"Who are your friends?" I asked the man beside me.

"That's my business. Let's just say that as long as Colby stays away from bad influences like you, he'll have those kids. If he loses them, he'll have only you to thank. I wonder how much he'll want you then, the man who made him lose those kids. You want to be responsible for that, Champagne? Is it worth a fast fuck? Anyway, Colby will deal. You can't be that good in bed."

"How would you know?" I met his gaze.

He didn't reply.

I sneered at him.

I was sure the Texas Crushers or the mob were responsible for this. The mob's probably already muscling in on the drug action with the Crushers. It wasn't enough for those bastards to have a piece of the drug pie, they wanted it all now. I'd tried to make peace between us. Damn it. I knew it wouldn't last, not with all that money up for grabs. Badger was so damn weak. He'd made a deal with the devil, the Texas Mafia. Everyone would pay now.

"There's a contract on me," I said, folding my arms across my chest.

"You're never getting out of the Banni, Diego, unless it's in a box."

I nodded. "Now tell me something I don't know."

"I suggest this little conversation stays between us. Colby has enough to worry about with those kids. He's out now.

Don't drag him back down into the dirt with you."

"Who else knows about Colby and me?"

"Your soldiers all think you're God's gift to women. I suggest you fuck that little girlfriend you keep on a string more often. She says you're one hell of a lover."

Tammy?

"There's a stool in my club. Who is it?"

No answer. I turned my head to look at Flint, and he was already on his way over to Colby. I watched him as he introduced himself and shook hands.

Colby loved those kids so much. He'd just buried his sister, and the other one was in prison. I couldn't mess it up for him. Didn't matter how much I loved him. And now there was a price on my head. If the Crushers or the mob wanted to get to me, they would eventually. But before they threw dirt over me, I was going to find out who had betrayed me and how in hell they knew that Colby and I were lovers.

I turned to go. Nuts was there, leaning against a tree nearby. He nodded at me. "They found the kids?"

"Yeah," I said.

"Looks like a mob hit."

I paused, stared at him. "Are you really sucking that cop's dick or what?"

He looked shocked. "Who said that?"

"I did. I said it." I started walking.

Nuts scrambled after me. "Who was that man, the one talking to you?"

"DCFS. I want you to find out everything you can about that fucking fat bastard. Follow him everywhere he goes."

Nuts struggled to keep up. "What's going on?"

I stopped. "How long you been putting it to that cop?"

"I'm . . . well . . . Diego, it's just fooling around, guy stuff, doesn't mean anything. You gonna tell the brothers?"

"No," I said. "Just knock it off."

He looked down at the sidewalk.

"And stop following me. Follow him." I hooked my thumb toward the scene.

"Diego!"

I glanced up to see Colby walking toward us. I swore under my breath. I looked at Nuts. "Go on, and don't say anything to Colby about anything."

Nuts nodded and walked toward Colby. He stopped, placed a hand on his shoulder. "Glad you found the kids." Then he kept on walking.

Colby met my gaze. "Where are you going?"

"You better pick up those kids."

"What do you think?"

"About?" I looked around.

"Diego. What's wrong with you?"

"Nothing. Listen, go and look after your family."

"When are we going to see each other?"

I looked around again.

"Stop fucking doing that," Colby snapped. He reached up and placed a hand on my face, turned it toward him. "Look at me."

"I'm looking. What am I supposed to be seeing?"

"The man you love." He swallowed. "You do love me. You even said it once." He stroked my cheek with his fingers. "You can act like an ass if you want, but it's in your eyes. You can't hide what's in your eyes."

I pushed his hand away. "Do you know who I am, Colby? Do you even realize what I am?"

Colby narrowed his gaze.

I rubbed my eyes. "I'm tired. I need to sleep." I turned to go.

Colby grabbed my arm.

I didn't look at him. "Let go of me, Colby."

"I can't. I won't. Never."

I placed my hand over his. "You have to." I looked at him.

"I'm no good for you. You're out of the Banni now so stay away from me." I gently removed his hand from my arm.

"So you leave me with all this? Alone? Someone killed those people and—"

"You don't need to worry about that." I took a few steps away. "Leave that to me. I'll figure that out. You're not in danger. Neither are the kids."

"What do you know that you're not telling me?"

"Colby. Forget it," I insisted. "Forget me." I turned and walked away. I wanted to run really, run as far away from Colby as I could.

He didn't follow. Thank God. If he had, I might have fallen on my knees and begged him to forget everything I'd just said. Damn it, why did he have to single me out that day when I was on my way to the bike rally? Why did he have to wake me up? If I could learn how to stop wanting him . . . stop loving him. If things were different . . . But they weren't, and I wasn't one to engage in fantasies.

I went back to the clubhouse. I didn't speak to anyone. I just went into one of the back rooms and crawled onto the bed. I closed my eyes. I wasn't sleeping. I couldn't sleep. My mind was racing. What did I want? It wasn't this. What I really wanted, I couldn't have. My life was a mess again, and it was about to get even messier.

I sat up. I wasn't going to walk around with my head ducked. I'd do what I'd always done, meet my fears head-on. But not yet. Tonight, I was going to get drunk, drunker than I'd ever been before. I was going to drink Colby right out of my mind.

When I came out into the bar area, some of the guys were there playing pool. Tammy was sitting with Jennifer, one of the dancers from the club. She was young. Her skirt was way too short, and she had on far too much makeup.

I nodded at the ladies and walked up to the bar. Marcel

immediately came over with a beer. I shook my head. "I'm going to need more than that tonight."

"Whiskey," he said, reaching under the bar. He poured some whiskey in a glass, then went to remove the bottle.

I shook my head. "Leave it."

Marcel's eyes widened a little, but he didn't say anything. I drank down the first and went for a refill.

Tammy and Jennifer were suddenly standing on either side of me. I glanced at Tammy. "What's this?"

Jennifer's hand slid down in front of me and rubbed my thigh then knuckled my cock. "You're a big boy."

I looked at her. "You think you can take care of me, do you?"

"I'd sure like to try." She tongued my ear.

"Jennifer," Tammy said. "I might be willing to share, but remember, Diego, is mine."

I poured more whiskey and drank it down. "You think?" I looked at Tammy.

She reached up and touched my hair. "Would you like that tonight? Both of us? You could handle us."

"Who did you tell I was good in bed?"

"What?" Tammy looked confused.

I turned around and grabbed her. I think I shook her a little.

"Diego," Marcel said. "What'cha doing?"

"Who did you tell?" I demanded.

She was crying. "No one . . . Jennifer, that's all."

I let her go. I turned to Jennifer. "Who asked you, someone at the club?"

"I don't . . . remember." She shook her head.

"Yeah, you do. Tell me."

Jennifer took a step back. "It was some guy . . . I don't know . . . he asked me if I'd ever . . . you know . . . had sex with you. And I said, yeah . . . and you were good."

I narrowed my eyes. "When did we have sex?"

"You don't remember." She looked hurt. "Guess I shouldn't have expected it. You were drunk. Like now. You fucked me right there on that pool table."

"I'm sorry," I said then went back to my bottle.

"Why? It was hot," she said, coming closer. "You want to do it again?"

"He's not fucking you without me being there." Tammy grabbed her arm and pulled her away.

I looked at Jennifer. "Don't you have any self-respect? What are you doing here hanging out with a bunch of bikers? None of these guys give a damn about you. I don't give a damn about you." I took the bottle.

Tammy was staring at me.

"That goes for you, too," I told her and went back to that room.

It was cold, dark, lonely and miserable. That's exactly what I felt like.

The door opened, and Tammy stood there.

"Go away," I told her.

"Diego."

"Tammy, can't you see I'm drunk? I'm not nice when I'm drunk. I'm not nice when I'm sober either. Find yourself a nice guy and leave me alone."

"I can't. I love you."

I wanted to scream. *No, no, no. Don't love me. Please. I don't love you, Tammy. I never will.*

I heard her crying and then she was gone. I drank down the rest of that bottle, then threw it against the wall. The last thing I heard was the glass shattering.

I must have passed out because Nuts woke me a few hours later. I wasn't in a good mood.

"Hangover?" he asked, chuckling.

"Go fuck yourself," I told him.

He laughed even harder and sat on the bed.

"What are doing on my bed? Get off, you pervert."

He stood. "You want the news?"

I put my face in my hands. I had a pounding headache. "Go on."

"Well, fatty took Colby to get the kids. He dropped them off. Then he went to Mickey D's and ate like five big hamburgers with a double order of fries and a milkshake and—"

"Nuts, please! I'm going to be sick. You don't need to tell me everything he ate. Where did he go after he stuffed himself?"

"Well, I thought he was going home. He went into this house, way out in the burbs. After a while, other cars started to arrive. Some kind of a meeting. "

I glanced at him. "And?"

"I managed to speak to a guy who came out of there. He looked upset. I stopped him and asked him what happened. He told me it's some sort of religious group. They invited him, but it wasn't what he expected."

"Okay."

"It was a cult meeting, a group of fruitcakes that call themselves Only the Righteous. Ever heard of them?"

"Ultra-rightwing, anti-everything."

"Basically . . . and although this guy told me he's in agreement with all that shit, he was scared."

"Of what?"

"He says they use violence, that they consider themselves to be angels of God."

I just stared at him.

"Then guess who I see coming outta there?"

I waited.

"Vinnie Carloota."

"Texas Mafia." Vinnie Carloota. Affectionately known as the Axe. The guy was the godfather's henchman, named so because he loved to cut up his victims with . . . you got it . . . an axe.

"Right."

"There's my connection." I got to my feet. Swayed a bit, then righted myself. "Jennifer still here?"

"You don't want that tonight boss, she's been had by half the club unless you're into sloppy seconds."

"Don't be disgusting." I headed for the door. My boot crunched on something.

"You smashed a bottle," Nuts pointed out unnecessarily.

"Fuck," I muttered, walking into the main hall.

Jennifer was parading around, waving her tits in everyone's face. "Who wants some?"

I reached out and grabbed her.

"Anytime, baby." She licked her lips.

I held up my hand, and someone threw me her blouse. "Put it on. I wanna talk."

She looked annoyed, but she got dressed quickly. "You sure are hot, but you're not any damn fun."

I scowled at her and motioned for her to come outside with me. It was nice to take the air.

"Tammy says you're finished with her. I wanna be your ol' lady, Diego." She tried to rub my thigh.

I shook my head. "I don't want a woman. Tell me one thing. Did you talk to a guy called Vinnie Carloota about me?"

"Vinnie? He's a big tipper."

"Jennifer . . ." I looked at her. "Focus. Why were you talking to Vinnie about me? Was he asking about me?"

Jennifer nodded. "I just told him you were Tammy's guy and she said you were good in bed, that's all. Did I do something wrong?"

"No. Tell me what else? Did you fuck him? Did he take you somewhere?"

"I went to a party at his house."

"Who was there?"

"Just Vinnie and . . . well . . . a few other guys I'd never seen before. I danced for them. They all fucked me, paid me well. Oh, yeah." She laughed. "Calvin and Cledus dropped by."

"And Cledus?" Why am I not I surprised? He'd chosen the best way to pay me back, to take away from me what I valued most, Colby.

"Yeah. It was before Cledus got sent up."

"Um. Okay." I had already surmised that. "And what happened?"

"Don't know. The two of them went into the other room and talked for a bit, then Cledus left." She leaned against the rail. "You gonna fuck me or not, Diego? You're really hot, hotter than any of the other guys here."

I fished in my jeans for my keys. "I gotta go."

She reached out to me. "Diego. Where? Let me come."

"Go inside, Jennifer," I told her. I went back into the club, stepped behind the bar and grabbed another bottle. With that in hand, I returned outside and headed down the steps. I threw the bottle into my saddlebag and straddled my bike. I had a momentary lapse of guilt concerning Tammy earlier. I'd been really cold, but I was too damned angry at Cledus to think about it much right now. I wanted to kill him. I could have someone on the inside do it but what was the point? He was in the hospital wing of the Big House, already dying.

Anyway, I was going to Texas, which would accomplish two things, it would give me an opportunity to meet with Badger face to face, and it would take me far away from Colby, which is where I really needed to be at the moment.

I stopped at a gas station and paid to fill the tank when my cell phone rang. It was Colby. I stared long and hard at it. I turned off the ringer and pocketed the phone. "Be happy baby," I said softly.

With the tank full, I sped off again. It was almost eleven at night, quiet on the roads. There was a brisk breeze, but I didn't mind. It kept me alert. I loved riding at this time of night with light traffic and no sun. I felt almost as if I were worry free.

When I saw the exit, I almost didn't turn off. I thought about driving until this damn bike was on empty, then hurling it over the embankment, myself along with it. I pulled over before I hit the city and got off the bike. I was still hungover. I almost regretted coming here, and I felt as if I was about to crash and burn.

I didn't care about the Banni anymore, or who had their hands on the drug trade. I was just going through the motions. I knew where I wanted to be, but now that I'd made that decision, it was no longer possible. Things had changed. Colby's life was forever altered. He had a family to raise and a business to run. It looked like somehow all the pieces of his life were coming together, while my life, on the other hand, was falling apart. I didn't know who I was anymore. I just knew I was lost. And the only place I'd ever really been connected to myself was when I was connected to Colby. And yet, I was the last thing he needed in his life.

Yep. I was feeling sorry for myself, and the only way to climb out of this dark hole was to get angry. So, I got back on my hog and nursed that anger all the way into Dallas.

I got a hotel room downtown. I asked for single bed, figuring I should get used to it. Desk clerk said they only had doubles.

Some rent boy tried to pick me up in the lobby, which should give you an idea of how many diamonds or stars this place had. I paused, gave the guy the once over. Something about him reminded me of Colby. "How much?" I asked him.

"You want the works, baby?"

"What? Are you a whore or a pizza?"

He laughed a little too hard.

Give me a break. It wasn't that funny.

"Anything you want." He licked his lips. "I'll charge you sixty."

"I'll give you a hundred." I didn't wait for him. I walked down the hall.

He chased after me. "I'd have to see the money up front," he said over my shoulder. I put the key in the lock.

I had shoved my colors in my duffle. Some hotels won't rent to bikers. He didn't know who I was. I wanted to keep it that way. I pulled out my wallet and showed him a wad of bills. I eyed him. "You rob me, and you'll be eating through a straw. Get it?"

"I got it," he said as he followed me into the room. "You're not Mr. Romance, are you?"

"I didn't pay for romance," I said, throwing my bag on the bed. I took the Jack Daniels out of my bag, stripped off my shirt and my boots, and hopped on the bed. I unscrewed the cap and took a few deep swallows.

"So, what's your name?" the rent boy asked, coming over to the bed. He trailed his gaze over my chest.

"Not important."

He reached out and touched my bicep. "My God," he said softly.

"Don't touch me until I tell you to." I eyed him. "And only where I tell you to. Take your clothes off."

He was stripping, and I was drinking. He was naked in a flash. Too skinny. Didn't these guys eat? Jesus.

"You're not going to be able to get it up if you keep drinking."

"What do you care? You'll get paid anyway. And it takes more than this stuff to stop me from getting an erection."

35

"What do you like?" He licked his lips.

He was on the bed now.

"Quiet, silence," I said softly. "I like . . ." I stopped and looked at him. "Colby."

"Who's Colby?"

"Nobody." I drank some more. "Undo my pants. Suck my cock."

Eager fingers reached over and unzipped my pants. "You're so . . . um . . . .so nice. Big, thick. Fuck me?"

I looked at him. I think I saw double. "Suck it."

I felt his lips wrap around my shaft and I grunted, digging my fingers in his hair. "Colby," I cried out. "Oh yeah, yeah. Go, go . . . I love you. I love you so much."

I gripped the bottle as I came hard. Hands moved up over my chest. I felt lips and tongue across my flesh. Someone moaned against my ear. "Hot . . . you're hot."

I woke up, and the sun was shining. I was covered in sweat and come and lying on the floor. A few minutes later when I was able to move, I found my wallet gone, along with my phone and the keys to my bike. It was not a good way to wake up. That little bastard had ripped me off big time. I let out a roar of anger. *Fuck, fuck, fuck!*

I told myself to calm down. I took a shower, got dressed and grabbed my bag. The bottle of whiskey was still on the nightstand. There was no more than a glass left in it. I slugged it back and left the room.

It was a different desk clerk, and I saw him smooth his hair when he saw me. Young, in the closet for sure, because his gaze settled on the bulge in my jeans and never left it until I crossed the floor. "You seen that rent boy that hangs out here?" I gave him a description.

That clerk smirked. "Was he in your room?"

"Yeah. I took pictures, wanna see?"

His smile faded. "His name is Albert. He rents a room

across the street."

"Oh, you mean at the hotel that's even more of a dump than this one?"

He nodded. "I guess."

"How convenient. At least he doesn't have to commute to go to the job. I'm checking out." I put the keys on the counter.

"Was everything to your satisfaction, Sir?"

"Well, the sex on demand was convenient except the little bastard robbed me."

"Should we call the police?"

I laughed. "Honey," I told him, "when I get done with him, he's gonna be calling the police." I walked out of the hotel, my bag over my shoulder, and dodged traffic to get to the other side. The hotel, ironically, was called The Torpedo. I had a momentary flash of Colby touching me. I winced.

It should have been called Rent Boy Central. I had to literally squeeze past several male hookers to get to the lobby. I got a lot of offers. None I cared to accept. I walked up to the desk.

The sleazy balding creep behind the bar came around and looked me up and down. "Nicely muscled, looks like you have a bubble butt. You ah . . . packing for real or you pad?"

I met his gaze. "Oh, it's all me."

"Good. Nice face, too. Tall. You want a job? I know a few brave clients that would take you on."

I reached out and grabbed the front of his shirt. I slammed him against the wall. His eyes widened. "You listen to me. I'm looking for Albert. He took my money, my phone, and my bike, all of which better still be here."

"You didn't come for a job." The guy shook his head.

"No. I have one. I'm Diego Champagne."

"Oh . . . oh . . . fuck me," he squeaked. And he didn't mean it in a good way.

I released him.

He was shaking like a leaf. "I'll ah . . . take you to him. He's sleeping upstairs."

"Tell me what room. I'll go myself. I like surprising people."

"Ah . . . six. He's in six."

"And where is my bike?"

"He parked it in the alley."

I didn't stay for more small talk. I ran up the stairs and found door six. I banged on it furiously.

My rent boy opened it a crack. "Oh, hello there, Albert," I said between clenched teeth and pushed through the door.

"Couldn't stay away?" He grinned.

"My keys, my wallet, and my phone . . . now." I put my hands on my hips.

"I was going to return them." He walked to the nightstand and handed them over.

"Right." I opened the wallet and counted the money.

"It's all there. I didn't even take my fee."

I counted out five twenties and threw them on the bed. "For services rendered."

"I'd do you for free."

"How generous." I turned to go.

"I wouldn't have stolen from you if I'd known who you were. Why didn't you tell me you were the leader of the Banni?"

"You didn't ask," I replied.

"Colby told me."

I sucked in some air and turned to look at him. "Colby?"

"I answered your phone."

"Fuck," I said under my breath. "You had no right."

"I had to. He left you many messages, all of them telling you how much he loves you. He really does, you know."

"And what did you tell him?"

"I told him the truth."

I closed my eyes.

"I told him I wanted you to want me, to fuck me, because last night you were so beautiful and hard and sexy. And that you were drinking a lot and I started touching you, and you called me Colby. You said you loved me over and over. You passed out, and I stayed there on that bed with you, looking at you, touching you. I even kissed your mouth, but you didn't know. I imagined you were mine 'cause most of the clients I get are dirty old men and monsters."

"How did I end up on the floor?"

"You woke up eventually." He smiled.

"I don't want to know," I told him.

"Okay," he said softly.

"Goodbye, Albert," I said.

"Colby cried a little."

I looked at him, my hand tightening on the doorknob.

"He told me how he'd never loved anyone until you, how he'd never fuck a guy more than once, but with you after the first time you were inside him, he never wanted to stop fucking you."

My vision blurred. I bit back the tears and forced myself to walk out of there. Downstairs I checked my phone. The battery was low. I didn't want Colby to cry, least of all over me. I pressed speed dial for his number.

"Diego." He answered in two rings.

"Were you sitting on top of the phone?"

Silence.

"Colby."

"What do you want me to say?"

"That you understand why we can't be together."

"I know it's complicated, but right now what I don't understand is what you were doing with another guy in a hotel room."

"Come on. Jesus, this isn't high school."

"You really want to fuck another guy?"

"No. And I didn't fuck him." I don't think. Didn't matter. It meant nothing.

"If you didn't, it was only because you were too drunk."

"No. It was because I love you too goddamned much."

Silence.

I rubbed my eyes. I was tired.

"What are you doing in Texas?"

"Line dancing."

He laughed for the first time. "Fuck off."

I laughed with him, too. "How are the kids?"

"Fine. Good. But not me. I'm not good. I need you. I'm not going to make it without you."

"Yes, you are going to make it. I need some coffee."

"Will you answer your phone if I call?"

"No. My battery is almost dead."

"There has to be a way for us, Diego. Please say there is."

"I don't know that way, baby. I'm sorry. Right now, I have a lot on my mind."

"Your mom is staying with me a while."

"Good," I said. "You can help each other. Bye, Colby." I hung up, then turned off the phone.

I drove to the nearest diner. I ordered some breakfast but couldn't eat much of it. I drank a gallon of coffee. After I paid the bill, I used the pay phone in the back to call Badger. It was almost two in the afternoon. A woman answered. One of his many girlfriends I presumed. "Let me talk to Badger."

"You have a sexy voice," she told me. "Badger, a sexy voice is on the phone for you, honey."

"Are you losing it, woman?" I heard Badger bark. "Get your skinny ass outta here." He took the phone. "Hey, what's up, homie?"

"Hello, Badger."

40

"Diego?"

"Surprised to hear from me?"

"No, man, of course not. What can I do you for? I'm at your service."

"Cut the shit. I want to meet."

"You here in town?"

"Yeah."

"Why, man?"

"We need to talk about the mafia and what they're doing in this drug deal. I thought you and I were square, man?"

"We are . . . we are square, cuz," Badger insisted.

"Why'd you stab me in the back then?"

"I didn't do that. My friend, I would never —"

"Then what's Vinnie got to do with it? The mafia's got a contract on my head."

"I didn't know. I swear." He whistled through his teeth. "No shit."

"Yeah, no shit," I repeated. "They give you a better deal?"

"It's just that it's on Texas soil, my man . . . you know how it is?"

"The Banni own the operation. The mafia needs to negotiate with us."

"That's real . . . ah . . . sticky. You see it's just Vinnie right now."

"What do you mean? Vinnie hasn't told the family?"

"No. It's a little side deal. As long as we go along, he'll keep the rest out of it. Otherwise, we'll lose control, you know? I didn't have a choice."

"So get rid of Vinnie, and you're clear of the mob."

"No way I kill a mafia guy. The mob has a way of knowing shit. They'll wipe us out. Not smart, Diego."

It was then it came to me, a way to put this life behind me once and for all. But it was going to take some planning, and I was going to need Badger's help. No one, not even Colby or my mother, could know the truth if I was going to make this work.

"You still there, homie?"

I wish he'd stop calling me homie. What a moron. "Listen, we need to meet, just the two of us. I have a proposition for you."

"Oh yeah?"

"This will keep the mob out of gang business and puts the Crushers in total control of everything."

"And what about the Banni? How much is this going to cost me?"

"One million dollars and you use the Banni for running only."

"One million and we retain control? That's peanuts, man. What's the catch? It's not my fucking birthday."

"The catch is, you have to kill me."

He laughed. "Diego, I would if I could, man. God knows I've tried. But damn it, you won't let me."

"Meet me in an hour. I'll tell you how you can strut around with a big erect ego."

"You're on."

I told him to leave his bike a block away and meet me in a nearby park under a shady tree. Then I hung up.

About an hour later, more or less, Badger strutted over to where I sat on a bench and took the place beside me. He looked straight ahead. "I came because I'm super curious. Why all the cloak and dagger stuff, hombre?"

I wanted to roll my eyes. Hombre now? "Is Vincent in Dallas?"

"I don't know. He's been saying some shit about you."

"I don't give a fuck what that bastard says about me."

"Okay. So, what's up with all this, Diego?"

"You earn a reputation as being the one to finally take down Diego Champagne, and the Crushers get a monopoly on the drugs."

He narrowed his eyes. "And what about Vinnie?"

"I'll take care of him for you."

"Why would you double-cross your club, man, and what about when your club finds out I'm the one who iced you?"

"The bragging comes later after the club thinks I sold them out. They won't avenge a traitor. It's in the code. In the beginning, they'll think my killer is someone in the Texas Mafia, retaliation for me killing Vinnie."

"You want to fake your death." His jaw fell. He met my gaze.

"Yeah. That's exactly what I want to do. We're going to need a body."

"No sweat. There's always one of those lying around, someone about your height and weight. We'll even remove the teeth."

"And burned beyond recognition, it won't matter. Only Nuts gets an anonymous call and directions to where to find my remains. My vest and hog will be there in the woods. He'll believe it's me. He knows I'd never leave my jacket or my bike. Nuts will tell the others I'm dead."

He looked at me, stunned. "You really want out. You got it all, man."

"Depends on your point of view, so, listen up." I leaned closer. "Here's the first thing I want you to do."

CHAPTER THREE

Colby

After the bloodbath at the Calhoun house, I was deter-
mined to move out of the new house on Coliseum. I felt
we were sitting ducks. We had no security, and we needed a
place that the bad guys, whoever they were, knew nothing
about. My realtor assured me we would find an immediate
buyer and she began searching for something move-in ready
with security doors and windows. A fortress would have
been nice.

I was forced to deal with the creepy Elmer Flint, who
wanted to know everything about my movements. He ques-
tioned me so closely I was surprised he didn't ask what color
underpants I was wearing. I felt bad about uprooting the
kids again. Life had been so traumatic for them lately, but
they seemed mesmerized by the adventures they'd been
having and judging by their responses to the female police
officer's questioning, they had no idea that their play date at
the Calhoun house had turned into the scene of multiple
homicides.

"Where is Miss Welda?" Little Garnet wanted to know. I
didn't know how to tell her that our caseworker was dead.

"She's on vacation," I told her. In time, she would learn
the truth.

"Is she coming back to us?" Garnet's gaze held a gravity
no little girl should know. I decided to tell her the truth.

"No, baby. She is not."

"That's good. She does talk about Jesus too much. Why does she say He doesn't love me? I know He does. And Henry, too." She gestured to the little guy, who nodded up at me solemnly.

"She told you that?" I was incredulous. We weren't religious zealots, but the kids went to church, and they observed our local church traditions. Since when did DCFS preach about God, anyway? And why would a decent adult talk this way to two kids who'd been through so much?

"Jesus loves you," Elmer Flint told Garnet.

She beamed up at him.

The guy creeped me out, but at least he wasn't trying to demean my children. He seemed quite taken by them and fully endorsed my plan to rent a house several streets away from where we'd been living. He promised to keep our location quiet. The last thing I wanted was more fruitcakes coming after us. And besides, I had no idea who'd been behind the attacks. And why.

Jennifer O'Dare, the realtor I'd been dealing with on the new house, told me we had an offer for almost twice what I'd paid for it. Man, oh man. The new paint on the walls wasn't even quite dry yet, and we were moving on.

I told Jennifer that I'd accept the offer. I hired a crew that came in and packed everything for us, taking it all to the new place on Constance Street. I wanted Garnet and Henry to have everything in the same place in their new rooms. The house was new, in the fake antebellum style that's suddenly become popular, but it blended with the other homes on the street.

The children liked the new place, and their rooms. Kids crave the familiar, and in the rental house, Cherise and I worked to make their rooms comfortable.

Painted a pale sage green with a dark green door and white trim, Garnet said the new house reminded her of a dollar bill.

"It looks like money," she said, making me and Cherise laugh.

The kids took the move in stride, accepting my explanation that we were offered a lot of money to sell. We were still right near Garnet's school on Coliseum, so she was happy. Henry was attending a local pre-school three days a week, but neither child complained when I kept them out of classes for a few days.

When they resumed their normal activities, I was able to focus on Cherise. And nurse my gigantic, aching feelings for Diego. I felt like he'd gone. Our last impassioned phone conversation had convinced me he loved me. He'd stopped talking to me, but he'd stopped speaking to his mother, too.

"I know my son, and he's up to something," she said. "Probably working on revenge for this." She indicated the new house. I took comfort in that. If he'd met someone new, he wouldn't ignore his mother. Maybe he'd made a dumb mistake with the whiny rent boy, but I didn't think he had displaced me in Diego's affections.

Their first day back at their respective schools, Henry and Garnet seemed excited to see their friends again. Henry tugged at my sleeve.

"Don't forget to pick me up," he said. My heart almost broke. I'd always thought Judd was a great dad; that he picked up the slack for my sister who'd been busy running the bakery she owned. Since he'd been incarcerated, I'd learned that he frequently forgot about the kids. My sister had formed a network of trusted friends who could be relied upon to collect the kids when she couldn't find her husband. With the kids being so young, this involved a lot of phone calls with June Gold first having to track down a mom willing to take the kids until she'd finished work. Then she'd have to call the school verifying that she'd given permission for the other mother to take Garnet and Henry home with her.

Now they had me. And Cherise. She was fantastic with them. So was Sue-Ellen when she was around. Jerry popped in and out and played tea parties with Garnet and rough-housed with Henry. Somehow, we made it all work.

So, it wasn't difficult to promise Henry that I would not forget him, that I'd be back to collect him at two o'clock. "I'll take you out for ice cream," I promised.

"What about me?" Garnet asked, her grave, pleading eyes tearing into my soul. She was so much like her aunt, my beloved sister, that I hunkered down.

"We'll all have ice cream," I promised. "Now, give me the biggest hug you can."

The kids threw themselves into my arms. Garnet, Cherise, and I walked Henry into his classroom, where his teacher was preparing a batch of plaster of Paris so they could make handprints.

I'd forgotten Father's Day was coming up. It had never, ever been important to me, but Henry hugged my leg now.

"I'm making your present today!" he shouted and ran off to join his little friends.

"He's so immature." Garnet sighed.

Immature? He was three! I squeezed her hand in mine. She squeezed back, then Cherise and I walked her to school. She was a sweet little girl, commenting on everything. She sometimes did not stop talking. I knew her parents rarely listened to her, and it hurt to know that June had always resented her. Garnet just wanted to be loved and held, to know that she mattered.

Cherise stroked her hair. She'd made pin curls for Garnet, who loved them. She was a proud girly-girl, who liked dolls and dresses, but more than anything, loved spiders. I had no idea how this obsession flared, but Jerry encouraged it since he adored spiders himself. The two of them could pore over picture books of tarantulas and other bugs. Her Bible was *Be Nice to Spiders*. She had been begging me for a terrarium and a spider for weeks. I'd have to cave in soon or get used to her dragging in anything with multiple hairy legs that she found at the bottom of the garden.

Once we dropped her at school, I put my arm around Cherise. "Your turn, lady."

"Will you buy me ice cream, too?" she asked.

"If you're a good girl, yes," I teased.

She smiled at me. "Oh, but I'm never good, Colby."

We turned a corner, and I could have sworn I'd spotted Calvin following us. How odd. He'd taken off on foot down an alleyway. We stopped. Why the hell would he be on our tail? I hadn't seen him since the District Attorney had indicted him on tampering with criminal evidence charges in connection with my sister's death. He'd been the one who'd driven her body to Alabama and tossed her remains in the forest. He'd escaped being held in custody until his trial for some obscure reason. I heard he'd offered to turn state's evidence against my father and sister, which surprised me.

My father had been his lover for many years, but still, Calvin had helped June and Cledus do away with Garnet Beauty.

"He's still following us." Cherise shook her head and sighed.

"What? You mean I'm not imagining things?"

Her face took on a hard caste. "No. He's called me a couple of times. He feels like he's lost his family, Colby."

"I have nothing to say to him."

She turned her gaze from me back to the street as we walked to her oncologist's office on St. Charles. "He wants to make amends. You and the kids are all he has."

"God, how disgusting. He threw my sister's body away."

48

"He thought it was an animal's body."

"What?" I turned to stare at her.

Cherise shrugged. "He thought, well, at least, that's what Cledus told him, that he'd accidentally killed the family dog and he was disposing of the body. Cledus said that the girls would be upset."

"Oh, my God. And you believe him?"

"I'm just telling you what he told me." Her body stiffened. "I believe him. Colby, they've been lovers for many, many years."

"Yeah, I know that."

A beat. "Calvin has stuck by your pa, in spite of everything. All his shitty behavior, his selfishness, all of it."

She was right. In his own weird, very warped way, Calvin had sort of been there for me. Sort of. When I needed to talk to my father, it was Calvin I went to, always. He knew how to smooth things over and present my case to Cledus in a way that guaranteed he wouldn't berate or beat me.

I thought about their relationship. I wondered how much in love they still were. I recalled Calvin helping my dad on gang-related matters. He would also drop food around to me when Cledus vanished for weeks at a stretch. Dang. He'd been Cledus's go-to guy for decades. Maybe he had believed the dog story. Maybe he hadn't wanted to know the truth. As far as I could tell, there'd been numerous unsavory things Calvin had done for my dad over the years.

It struck me that keeping an eye on me had been all him, but maybe Cledus had said, "Take some cans of soup to Colby." It had been a distant kind of love from Calvin, the only kind some men can give. He'd never been the warm and fuzzy type, but in his own way, I had to grudgingly admit he'd cared about me.

"He's like Othello. How does it go exactly? One who loves not wisely, but too well." Cherise glanced up at me.

"We've all done it. He's just never been able to shake off your father. He'll go to his grave knowing he picked one hell of a lousy hand in the romance department."

I tried not to think about my last jarring conversation with Diego and hoped history wouldn't be repeating itself.

"He just wants to speak to you. I said I would mention it, but ever since the murders, he's been calling me. A lot."

I couldn't imagine what he might say to me. I was glad he hadn't come to the funeral, and I didn't want to hear any half-assed apologies. Sorry just wouldn't cut it. I said nothing. Cherise and I trudged the rest of the way in companionable silence and arrived at her doctor's office. The place looked packed when we went inside. Cherise became instantly nervous. She signed in, and I insisted she take the only available seat in the waiting room. I stood against the wall as she sat, leafing through an ancient copy of *People* magazine as though it were the most fascinating thing in the world. I became restless. Something made me walk across the room and look out the window. I wasn't too surprised to see Calvin across the road, looking at the building. He didn't seem to have noticed me. He whipped out his cell phone and made a call.

I turned, holding up a finger to Cherise, who caught my glance and nodded. I bolted from the room and out of the building. I covered the space between me and Calvin in several strides. He appeared startled when I barged right up to him.

"Who you talkin' to?" I demanded, half-fearing that the Texas Crushers would show up with machine guns.

"Jerry," he said, surprising me. His tone was mild, almost apologetic.

I blinked. I knew he and Jerry had been quietly screwing each other. I had no idea it was still going on. Or was it?

"He asked me to follow you. Keep an eye on you and the

kids," Calvin told me. Into the phone, he said, "Spider, baby, I'll call you back." A pause, and then a sickening smile. "Love you, too."

Oh, God. I wished I could have scrubbed the image of the two of them from my mind. There wasn't enough bleach in all the world. I shook my head.

"Why does he want you following me, and why didn't he mention it?" I was furious now.

"We're all on the skids with the Banni," he said. He fixed me with a hard stare. "Because of you. You just had to go diggin' up ancient history."

I gaped at him. "My sister was murdered."

He flapped his hands at me. "Yeah, yeah, I know. And frankly, mebbe it was the best thing that coulda happened to your old man. He's in a place where he's forced to get help. They want him to get better to stand trial. And, frankly, it's better for me. Jerry and I wanna be together. As soon as we feel you and the kids are situated, we're outta here." He glanced away from me. "As soon as the trial's over, of course."

"Does my dad know you're gonna testify against him?"

"No. And that's another thing. They're putting me in Witness Protection."

"What?"

"Your father has killed over three hundred people. I know where the skeletons are, literally, and frankly—" His cell phone rang.

Frankly. He seemed overly fond of the word. I tried to absorb what he'd told me. He seemed to be talking to Sue-Ellen.

"That's Sue-Ellen," he said, confirming my thoughts. "She's anxious to have you and the kids over for dinner. I said I'd invite you."

"You're all pretty chummy." I was trying to digest the

idea that my father was a homicidal maniac. The problem for me, though, was that Calvin had participated in at least some of those crimes, I was certain. I'd witnessed him and Cledus beating up one guy, leaving him paralyzed. Man, I really had been running around with some lethal assholes.

"Does Jerry know about Witness Protection?" I asked.

"He's coming with me. He has to figure out a way to tell Sue-Ellen. We've both broken away from the Banni. The gang scene's over for us, and I know it is for you, too. Jerry and I will be gone in another week, but neither of us feels safe."

"You're afraid of the Banni?" I tried to figure out why. Calvin had been involved with very little of their activities. Or, had he?

"I helped kill Purnell Torrens." Calvin's voice became a whisper. "The cops don't know, but I'm willing to sweeten the deal and throw him into the pile."

"Won't they arrest you?"

He gave me a sick grin. "No. I'll tell them Diego did it. He took part in the interrogation."

"Are the police interested in a low-level thug like Torrens?" I was worried for Diego now.

"Sure they are. Especially considering he was an undercover cop."

"And you're willing to perjure yourself?"

"Only if I have to."

"What do you want, Calvin? I don't buy your bullshit that you care about me and the kids."

"Aw, that hurts my feelings." His voice dripped sarcasm. "I want you and Diego to stay alive. There's a bounty on his head, and some asshole just made you pack up and run from your brand-new house."

"And this affects you how?"

"People are lookin' at me. Somebody hates you bad, Colby. You, and Diego. I don't like fingers being pointed at me. All our lives your dad and me kept our relationship secret. Real private. Five minutes after you get with that pup Diego, the whole fuckin' world knows your business! You're like an infectious disease. Man, even Nuts thinks he's a cock-tailer now."

I had to talk to Duchesne. He was a cop, but I trusted him.

Calvin shook his head. "Long as I'm here, I aim to keep you safe. I need you alive until me and Jerry can get outta here."

"And you want me alive to prove you're not trying to kill me?" I couldn't keep the sneer from my tone.

"Insurance. I got no real beef with you, apart from the fact you wouldn't let your sister disappear." He shrugged. "Once I'm gone, once I prove I ain't the one who's after you, I don't give a fuck what happens to you."

But you have no beef with me? Yeah, right. The man's morals were all over the map. I stared at him. When had he started hating me so much? It had just begun to sink in that he was taking Jerry away from here. From . . . me. And Sue-Ellen. She and Jerry were close. Closer than close. Man, she'd given up everything to raise him and had stuck by him through all our years in our former gang, Death Proof. We were all scattering to the winds. Looked like everybody was getting what they wanted.

Except me and Diego.

"I appreciate the watchful eye," I told Calvin, "but it's the mafia that wants Diego dead."

"They want both of you dead."

"Being gay isn't contagious, and it's not a disease."

He fixed me with a hard stare. His hatred for me seeped from his very pores. "I've disavowed any knowledge of Purnell Torrens' murder, but I know where the body is. One wrong word from you, sunshine, then I'll talk. I'll tell 'em

Diego did it and that you and Jerry cleaned up the crime scene on his orders."

"But you want to take Jerry away with you. If you say he was involved, won't that wreck your plans?"

"No." His tone turned cool, his eyes gleaming with mischief. "Not at all. He would tell the cops that the two of you cleaned up the crime scene. He'd point the finger at you." His grin turned feral. "He'd lay blame at your feet for other crimes, too."

Other crimes? I hadn't been involved in many. As the leaders of Death Proof, Jerry and I had run a tight crew. I think my father and Calvin resented that we didn't embrace mayhem the way they had when they were the top dogs.

Oh, man. I kept thinking about the Purnell Torrens killing. He had been Teresa's half-brother. At least, that's what I'd been told. Teresa had been Jerry's former fiancée, and she'd gone mad when Jerry tried to break things off with her. She owned a tomato farm, and he thought it gave him stability and the appearance of straight-dom having a biker chick for a fiancée. Meanwhile, he'd been screwing Calvin behind her back, and she'd figured it out.

She went mad. Absolutely crackers. In Austin, Texas, at the start of the bike rally where I'd first met Diego, she'd assaulted Jerry in a bar, almost killing him, and me, too. Diego had stepped in and saved my life.

Jerry had been in the hospital for weeks, and Diego and the Banni had protected us. It had been the end of Death Proof. Meanwhile, it transpired that the real reason Teresa wanted Jerry dead was that all the money he'd socked into her respectable fruit farm had been funneled into a gigantic marijuana operation.

The gangs have been fighting over it ever since.

Jerry and I went to confront Teresa after she attempted to kill us again but were surprised to find her vacuuming naked, in high heels, chatting with her lover, Chase. That had been a shock all right. Chase. Leader of the Banni. Of all people.

Teresa got out of control, and Chase blew her away right in front of us.

I don't think anyone missed that maniacal blonde, except that out of nowhere, her half-brother emerged during a time when another thug named Lafleur was after Diego.

Diego had tracked down and captured Torrens. He'd smacked him around and worked on him to get information about Lafleur's whereabouts, which, I recalled now, was in a bunker on Teresa's farm. But it was Calvin who went into the basement of that old building and killed the guy after beating him.

Calvin seemed dangerously happy now. "Yeah, you can see the bottom of your world falling out now. Not much fun, is it? Now you know how me and your pa feel."

"The bottom of my world fell out the day you, my father, and June conspired to kill my baby sister. You were in my life, Calvin. You can't say I had a happy childhood. But thanks for helping me ensure that my sister's kids might actually get to have one."

That shut his ugly mouth. He stared at me. I had to call Diego and tell him. I had to check with Duchesne about Purnell Torrens being an undercover cop.

"Have a nice day," I said when Calvin stopped speaking. I turned and crossed the road again, but he grabbed me just as a car screamed by, missing me by inches.

"Careful now," he teased. The chuckle in his voice sent chills down my spine.

"Thanks."

As I proceeded to cross, he called after me. "And leave Jerry outta this. If I find out you've been calling him, I'll make sure you regret it, Colby."

I'm sure you will. I kept walking and found myself shaking as I returned to the doctor's office. Cherise was still waiting, and she was leafing through a torn kids' book now.

"Everything okay?" she asked, her gaze anxious.

"Peachy." I gave her what I thought was a reassuring smile. Anyone who knew me well was aware that peachy meant anything but. My sisters had been named after Texas peaches. I shook my head. My niece, Garnet Beauty. She was named for my baby sister, who'd been named for my maternal grandpa's favorite peach. Maybe the kids and I would move to Texas. Back where it all began.

No. We'd move wherever Diego wanted us to go. He felt very far away from me now, but a future without him was impossible. One day. One day, we would make it.

I moved into the hallway and called him. I got his voicemail and left a message for him, hurriedly repeating my conversation with Calvin. I remembered cleaning up the crime scene, but it had been a sickening, furtive operation. I also knew that Calvin hadn't carted the dead man's body away. He'd taken Diego to the hospital after Stu got hold of a knife, aimed for Torrens, and apparently swung too wide and slashed Diego's face instead. Stu was one of the guys who got rid of the body. I simply could not recall who the other man was. I could have asked Jerry but didn't want to risk calling him and getting Calvin all pissed at me.

Back inside the office, Cherise was getting ready to meet with her doctor. She looked relieved to see me and seemed to age as she grasped my arm for comfort. We walked into the office. As we sat at the desk, Cherise went rigid until her doctor smiled. Now that was a reassuring smile.

"Your numbers are good, and the tumor has shrunk considerably, but I'd like to do four more weeks of chemo as we planned," he said. "The combination therapy is working very well." He turned over the blood test results to her, and I looked over her shoulder as she compared the report from earlier in the month to the current one.

Her new regime involved weekly chemo sessions, followed by hydration and platelet infusions the following day. She'd handled the first four weeks well but had hoped to avoid more sessions.

"I'm tired, and I've lost a bit of my hair," she whined. I shot her a look. We'd opted for the expensive cold cap method, which her insurance didn't cover. Diego and I had covered the cost of this aspect of her treatment because she was obsessed with keeping her hair. During chemo sessions, she would wear the helmet-like cap, which cooled her scalp, ensuring that her hair didn't 'burn' off. We'd had to purchase several caps because they needed to be changed every hour during chemo.

She had kept her precious tresses, but even losing a single strand could reduce her to tears.

Dear, sweet Cherise. She was fretting about follicles when I would have been more concerned with the other side effect she'd developed.

"She's lost her sense of taste," I blurted.

The doctor glanced from me to her. "Oh, Cherise, I'm so sorry. Some patients do experience that. Once chemo is completed, eighty percent of patients do recover their taste buds over time."

"What if I'm the twenty percent?" she asked.

"You're doing great," he said, "I have a feeling you will be fine."

Was he flirting with her?

Cherise smiled at him and fidgeted in her seat. My cell phone rang. I'd forgotten to turn it off. I checked the readout. A text. It was from Diego. I almost did the happy dance on the doctor's desk.

He gave her a hug as we left the office, and she practically skipped down the hall.

"My tumor's shrunk!" she called out to the receptionist, who gave her a thumbs-up. Half the waiting room did, too. It was a sweet moment. I hugged Cherise, who was teary-eyed with relief.

Out on the street, Calvin was doing a lousy job of secret surveillance.

Cherise seemed surprised to discover him lurking by a bus stop. "Didn't you talk to him?"

"Yeah, I talked to him. He says he's following us to protect us."

"That's what he told me, too. But he said he had something to discuss with you. Something about the future."

My whole body tensed, and I wished I could have walked over to him and popped him in the nose. He was really beginning to bug me. We had to wait for two buses and several cars before we could cross over. I pulled out my cell phone and checked my text message from Diego.

It read *He's an ass, and full of shit. Torrens was no cop. He was a dirty cop who did time. Not undercover. He's trying to freak you out and doing a good job. Look after Cherise. Kiss her and kids for me. xx*

Huh. No kisses for Colby. Always the bridesmaid, never the bride. I looked up just as I heard a man's screaming voice and a squeal of breaks. A sickening thud. Several people started to yell, and Cherise darted across the road to the group that had formed around the back of a bus.

The driver was wailing to anyone who'd listen. "I couldn't stop. It was crazy! That man came outta nowhere and pushed that man under my wheels! I drove straight over him!"

Under the wheels was the unmistakable, mangled form of Calvin.

"What man?" I asked.

The driver pointed, a look of confusion on his face. "He

was right there. Bushy fella."

"I saw him," one of the women in the group piped up. "He looked like a biker. Long beard. Ginger colored."

That sounded like Nuts.

Then I saw the scattered peanuts everywhere. Holy heck. Maybe it had been Nuts. But why?

He dropped his shopping everywhere," a woman said, gesturing to the nuts. He swung the bag at the man under the wheels. It was horrible."

A wail of sirens, and next thing I knew, Duchesne was walking up to the crime scene.

"You witnessed this?" he asked, shooting me a baleful glance.

"No." I shook my head. "We were at the doctor's office across the road."

"We heard it." Cherise lifted her shoulders. "But we were too late."

"If you didn't see it, you need to leave."

I took Cherise's arm and steered her away from there. I wondered if I should call Jerry and break the news to him. I wondered how he'd take it, since he and Calvin had been planning to take off together.

My cell phone rang as I walked with Cherise. I ignored the call when I saw it was a newspaper reporter's number. The same guy had been calling ever since the murders. I speed-dialed Jerry and broke the news to him.

"I have no idea who pushed him, but the driver says it was a guy with a beard." Silence on the other end. "You there, Jerry?" I asked, not expecting the sound that I heard.

CHAPTER FOUR

Diego

I regretted taking the call when I heard Cledus's voice. "How'd you get this number?"

He gave a weird chuckle. "I'm dyin' does it matter? I ain't passin' it on." His voice was raspy and weak, filled with pain and regret. If he'd been stronger, there would have been rage. He couldn't quite do rage. He didn't waste his time with greetings.

"You bastard," he hissed in the phone like a snake. "You vengeful, cock sucking, son of a bitch."

"Aren't you dead yet, Cledus?" I asked him without emotion.

My phone had rung just as I pulled off the highway at a rest stop. I'd gassed up, bought a coffee, and was sitting on a bench outside a McDonald's. It was warm today, and I'd unbuttoned my shirt. My vest was safely tucked away, and I felt quite normal, like any other young guy out for a spin on his bike. A call from Cledus was just icing on the cake, wasn't it?

It took Colby's old man a long time to respond to my question. Maybe he wasn't quite sure if he was dead or alive. He was literally wasting away from cancer.

Finally, he said some things I couldn't quite hear. I think he was crying at one time. It didn't move me at all. After what he'd put Colby through, and killing a kid, my compassion for the guy was at an all-time low. "Listen, Cledus,

60

there are professionals for that."

"Fuck you. Fuck, fuck, fuck you, Champagne. You took my Calvin."

"I didn't take Calvin anywhere. I believe it was a bus."

"You ordered the hit."

"I'm really afraid to disappoint there. Wasn't me."

"Do you really think my son deserves to be with a lowlife scum sucker like you?"

"No, I don't," I said honestly. "Colby isn't with me." I took a sip of my coffee. It was cold now. "You can damn me all you want, Cledus, and even pretend you are concerned for Colby's welfare. I don't give a shit. You'll be happy to know I'm on the run. There's a hit out on me. Texas Mob. I'm a dead man, just like you. Let's continue this conversation later in hell, shall we?" I hung up.

I squashed the paper cup and threw it into the garbage can then I did up the buttons on my shirt and walked over to my bike. A couple of teenage boys were fawning over my chopper, which had a 120-cubic-inch Accurate Engineering Outlaw panhead, dual SS carburetors, and a Baker six-speed transmission. This baby could hold the road. They backed off when they saw me. "It's cool," I said. "You like her?"

"Wow." One of the boys shook his head. "She's a beaut. She's got ego trip wheels, man. I saw one like that once."

"Custom made," I said. "Modeled after the Soul Shaker."

"Yeah, that was it," the boy said. "It was at one of those bike shows."

"Bet she rides like a dream," the other boy offered.

I grinned and straddled the bike. "You bet."

"You are a biker, like for real?" The other boy asked curious.

I roared the engine just to give the kids a thrill and shook my head. "Naw." I grinned. Then I lifted a hand and drove off.

A few miles down the road the loneliness set in. I was super melancholy. Usually, a ride on my bike, alone on the road, could fix that, but not this time. I missed my bike shop. I missed my mother, but most of all, damn it, I missed Colby. I missed holding him and talking to him. I missed the way he looked at me with desire and love in his eyes. All the rest of it I was more than happy to leave behind. I'd been gone almost nine weeks now, travelling around the Southwest, up to Arkansas, and down to New Mexico. Now, it was Oklahoma, all part of the plan to make everyone think I'd mysteriously disappeared. When they found the body, it would be unrecognizable and unidentifiable, and that's the way it had to be.

I'd thrown away my cell phone a long time ago so I wouldn't pick up if Colby rang, weaken, and speak to him. I'd jammed my colors into my saddlebag, and I had a substantial growth of beard.

Badger was my only contact, and, so far, I believe he was holding up his end of the bargain, though it still nagged in my mind how Cledus got my number. It didn't matter now. The man was dying and soon couldn't hurt anyone.

Badger kept me posted on Vinnie and watched over Colby, to make sure he wasn't being harassed and the kids were all right.

As for my mother, she was in good hands with Colby. Those two had just taken to each other. I could only imagine now what they were saying. I supposed they were both frantic over my whereabouts, and, yes, I felt bad having to put them through it. But I had no choice. I hoped it wouldn't affect my mom's progress, but she was strong.

A few hours later, I was in some drinking hole outside Oklahoma City. It was Saturday night, and I had nothing much to do. I was preparing to get wasted. Before that, I walked outside and used my disposable cell phone. It was time to call Badger for our weekly chat.

Badger knew the number and answered right away. We didn't waste too much time on niceties. Badger and I had never liked one another much, but we did have some mutual respect. That's why neither of us was dead. Right now, we needed one another, and it had always been that way, friends in need, enemies when our interests were in conflict. If we'd been lovers, the makeup sex would have included rockets going off. "Where is Vinnie?" I asked.

"He just bought a whorehouse in Little Rock Arkansas. He's going to be there for a few weeks, making sure the pimp is doing his job."

"I hear you. You got an address?"

"Give me a minute." He came back minutes later and rattled off an address. "You got that?"

"Yep. And you?"

"It's ripe, charbroiled, no teeth, and fingers cut off at the joints. Tell me I'm a genius."

I rolled my eyes. "Well done."

"And you'll let me know about our soon to be dearly departed friend?"

"As soon as it's over."

"Don't miss."

"I won't."

"Make sure he's not coming back."

"He won't."

"When can I expect you in Texas?" he asked.

"I'll swing down to Arkansas, then, when it's done, I'll head back up to Texas where I'll dump my personal effects. Give me a couple a days. I'll call you when I get there. I need to make sure I'm not seen. Have my money ready."

"You got it."

"Double-cross me, Badger, and I won't hesitate to kill you."

"I thought you trusted me, hombre?"

"I'll trust you more if you stop calling me that."

"Okay, man." He chuckled.

"How's my mother, Colby, and the kids?"

"Your mom has been out and about, shopping and shit. My contact says she looks good."

"Great. And the kids?"

"They go to school like normal brats. Colby gets them every day and works in the bakery, making cakes and shit. Same old, same old."

"Good. Those religious freaks are keeping their distance?"

"As long as Colby isn't fucking you, they seem happy."

"Glad they are," I muttered. "I'll be in touch."

"Be careful of those banjo-dueling ass fuckers, Diego." Badger laughed. "Oh yeah, forget it. I heard you like that sort of thing."

"Go fuck yourself," I told him and hung up. I leaned against the building and closed my eyes. I could hear the hillbilly music playing inside. Where in the hell was Creedence Clearwater Revival when you needed them?

These past few weeks had given me a taste of freedom like I'd never known. I wanted more of it. I wouldn't miss tensing up every time I saw a cop car or another biker gang. I didn't want to sleep with one eye open or step over dead bodies, or move coke, or . . . make money off prostitutes or fight every day to survive. I wanted to live my life with integrity, making a living doing beautiful custom bikes. I wanted to be with the man I loved, and I didn't want to hide it anymore. I couldn't wait to walk down the street and hold Colby's hand. Christ . . . I even wanted to marry the guy.

I smiled. Yeah. That's what I wanted. And if Colby would ever forgive me for the stunt I was about to pull, I'd get down on what was left of these damaged knees and propose. I'd give him romance and roses if that's what he wanted.

I walked back inside the bar and asked the barman for whiskey. "Keep 'em coming," I said, tossing back the first one.

I'd rented a room on top of that hillbilly bar and, some-how, I managed to crawl up the stairs and find a bed a few hours later. The damn sun was blinding me when I opened my eyes, and I groaned. I pulled a rough blanket over my head and ignored the spring that was poking my hip. Damn uncomfortable bed and the blanket smelled musty.

It didn't matter. I was leaving soon. I dozed off some more, then forced myself to get up. It was already noon, and I had a bad hangover. It was becoming a habit. I vowed that once this was over, once I could be with Colby again, I'd quit drinking altogether. But right now, it was the only thing keeping me sane.

Downstairs, I skipped the breakfast being served until one. When I saw the eggs swimming in grease with the grits and piles of dripping bacon, I almost hurled. I accepted the coffee and sat there drinking it. It was strong and raunchy, like Louisiana mud. It was bad, but it was exactly what I needed.

I didn't waste time getting back on the road. I really wanted to get this over with. How did I feel? Well, I was traveling alone on the highway, on my way to kill someone. I decided not to dwell on what I was about to do. Instead, I thought about what it would mean to be free of this life, and with Colby, tucked up together in some sweet little house somewhere with the kids. Maybe we could get another dog. Beauty, his beautiful pit bull, needed a companion. I thought about a place to live, some nice little town where it wasn't too 'red-necked.' Vermont, near the Canadian border, would be nice. I could set up a bike shop, and Colby could work with me, or do whatever he wanted to do.

The drive was a little over five hours. I got off the bike to gas up, have more coffee, and stretch my legs. I stopped for a burger about a hundred miles from Little Rock, but my appetite was nil. Planning to kill someone did that to a person, I guess. Not to mention, I'd been drinking too much. My stomach was screaming at me big time.

No matter how you justify murder, you come up short. I didn't even believe in the death sentence. Being who I was, I had good reason, I guess. And yes, I'd killed people, but it was always me or them. I wasn't proud of that, but it was a dangerous life. It's not like we didn't know what we were getting into. It was the price we paid.

I told myself that Vinnie was a bad guy. He'd killed tons of people, and he'd kill tons more before he was finished if I didn't take care of him. I was doing society a favor, wasn't I?

I knew Vinnie would shoot first when he saw me, and for my own peace of mind, I had to make it self-defense even if I was going to deliberately initiate the confrontation.

I hit Little Rock around six in the evening. One couldn't help thinking about the Civil Rights movement in this place. The desegregation of schools started here. Blacks fought for their rights to be treated as equals. To me, it didn't seem like a lot had changed for people of color in the South. They tell me it's better in the North, but I'm not so sure.

I cruised down the main drag on my bike, looking for a place to crash. It didn't have to be fancy, just clean and quiet. As I was scouting the signs, a name flashed in my brain. I turned at the next corner and drove around again just to be sure. I thought I'd imagined it but, no, there it was on the billboard. Live at the Little Rock Arena, Maurice Champagne against Reese Turner. Twelve Rounds.

I double parked the bike and got off. I read the sign again. Yep. Maurice Champagne. There was an arrow pointed down the side street. I walked like a drunk toward the building. The fight was on now.

I walked into the arena. I could hear the yelling and screaming coming from inside. I remembered the people screaming and yelling when I did extreme fighting. It sent a shiver down my spine.

A man behind a ticket counter motioned to me. "Going to buy a ticket? It's almost over. It's mind blowing, gone six rounds. He's not going to last much longer."

"Who isn't going to last?"

"Champagne. He's finished. Washed up. Reese should have knocked him out a long time ago, but he just keeps getting back up."

I smiled. Sounded like a Champagne. "Give me a ticket."

"Twenty-two-fifty."

I handed him the money. A big guy opened the door. I stood at the back, the glare of the lights blinding me a minute. I could see the two men in the boxing ring. One was dancing. The other was staggering. I knew which one my father was right away. He was taller than his opponent, well-muscled, with dark hair. He looked worn out. He kept jabbing at the air while the younger guy danced around him and got him on the ropes.

I walked up the aisle and took a seat on the end of the third row. It was hard to watch. Reese just kept hammering at him. Maurice went to his knees. There was so much blood covering his face, you couldn't see it anymore.

The ref was ready to call the fight. Reese waited, dancing around. The crowd roared. My father tried to get up. He stumbled, swayed, and Reese went for the kill. Two minutes later, the ref was calling, "Knock out."

It was all over. Two men in front of me said. "That Champagne. He wasn't going down easy. He used to be the best. Now, he's finished. I doubt he'll ever fight again."

Some old man was scraping my father off the canvas. He was walking, pushing the old guy away as he tried to wipe blood off his face. I was going to leave. I couldn't deal with this right now. I'd come here to kill a man, not have a reunion with my old man, whom I hadn't seen since I was like two or three. I could hardly remember. Then I thought of my mother. I recalled her telling me that he just didn't up and leave his family. He was sent to jail for a crime he didn't commit, labeled a rapist by a rich white lady in town whom he'd rejected. His mother had told him his father didn't want his son to be tainted by what had happened. But his father being absent hadn't done him much good either. He'd left him all the responsibility and, as a result, it had led him to exactly this place.

I took a breath and headed to the front. I walked around the ring, through the crowd that surrounded the champ and headed down a long hallway. Two men stood in front of a room at the end of the hall. "No fans back here," a big guy told me.

"I'm not a fan. I'm his son."

The man nodded, hooked his thumb toward the room. "Go ahead."

My stomach was in knots. I walked into the locker room to see the man who'd sired me sitting on a bench. An old man handed him an icepack. I was looking at my own face in twenty some odd years, hopefully, less ravaged. It was strange.

The old man stared at me. "What do you want, kid?"

Maurice Champagne looked up at me. He stared at me a long time, but he didn't say anything. I didn't either. I couldn't.

"Leave us, Louie," he said. In his voice was a smatter of an accent. Not French, not Spanish, not even Louisiana, but a combination of all three. That voice sounded so familiar. I remembered it.

The old man grumbled and walked away.

"Come here," Maurice said.

I took a few steps. "You know me then."

"Diego Champagne, leader of the Banni de Louisiane. Everyone knows you."

"Not anymore."

"Got smart, did you?"

He'd been handsome once, but the ravishment of a long fighting career had changed that.

"What are you doing here, Diego?"

"I've come to kill a man." My voice faltered.

"Does that man deserve to die?"

"Yes." I nodded. I was convinced of that.

"Are you his worthy assassin?"

"Don't play fucking philosopher with me." I didn't raise my voice, but the anger was there, simmering. "I hate you."

"Look at you. You're beautiful, big, tall and strong. I did something right I guess."

"Fuck you. You didn't do anything right."

"I've always loved you, Diego. I thought I was doing the right thing after I got out of the joint."

"You were a coward." I shook my head. "You left me to take care of her. And it ruined . . . ruined . . ." I choked now. I stopped and took a breath. I wanted to punch something. "You ruined my life." I turned to look at the wall because I couldn't stand to look at him.

"Forgive me." I heard him sobbing, and I couldn't comfort him. Frankly, I was running on empty. I had nothing left to comfort him with. I turned to look at him. His chest heaved. His head was lowered.

I had what I came for. I guess I needed to know he'd suffered too. "Bye, Dad," I said.

"Diego, wait," he said.

I turned and glanced at him.

"Don't get yourself killed."

My mouth twisted. "What do you care?" I left, walking as if in a dream. I could do it now. I could kill Vinnie.

I got on my bike, which by some miracle had not been ticketed, and headed to Vinnie's spanking brand-new whorehouse. I don't know why but, suddenly, after seeing my father, I realized that I wasn't immortal. My father must have felt that when he got into the ring tonight with that much younger fighter. Why did he do it? I guess because he had to, just like I'd had to fight to survive. And I had to kill Vinnie, too, and fake my death if I ever wanted a life. If I died, well it meant I'd failed. I couldn't fail.

I found the whorehouse easily. It was a triplex with black iron banisters at the end of a dead-end street. All three apartments were being used, windows open and music blaring. Pleasant as hell for the neighbors. Men were going up and down the stairs, and, every once in a while, I caught a glimpse of the women. Young, probably illegals. There was no expression on their faces except sadness.

I parked my bike in an alley and waited. My weapon was ready. It was no high-powered rifle with a zoom. It was a simple handgun, but it would do the job.

About an hour later, I saw what could only be described as two mafia thugs coming out of the upper apartment. Why did they always wear three-piece suits in the middle of summer? It boggled the mind. I guess they liked to dress for success. They were Vinnie's bodyguards. I knew Vinnie couldn't be far.

A small compact Ford sat parked on the corner. I watched the two men walk over to it. One checked inside, the other looked underneath. Satisfied the car wasn't rigged with a bomb, they took out cigarettes and lit up. One leaned on the hood of the car, and the other was waving his arms, obviously excited about something.

I was impatient. "Come on, Vinnie, come already, get your pants on, and get the fuck out here."

It was like he heard me because a few minutes later, I saw my intended victim walk out of the first-floor apartment. He strutted up the street, a right-wing hypocrite, fucking prostitutes in his spare time and going to confession on Sunday. I sneered. It was always like that.

I backed into the shadows as Vinnie got into the car with the two gorillas and they sped off. I jumped on my bike and followed at a safe distance. I had to find the right moment, a moment when Vinnie was away from the other two, and I could get to him. It wasn't going to be a cakewalk.

We didn't ride long. Apparently, the creep was hungry after fucking a few prostitutes. They pulled over in front of a fancy Italian place. Damn. With my scruffy appearance, I wasn't getting in that place soon.

I waited a block away. All three men disappeared inside. I drove slowly by the restaurant and around the corner. I checked out the back. The door to the kitchen was there. I could get in there but do what, wait for him to go to the can and do him there. No. It was too public and too risky. I'd have to wait until he came out and do a drive-by.

Three guns to my one, it wasn't going to be a party. Again, I played the waiting game. I parked my bike a block away, put on a pair of gloves, then looked around for a car that would be easy to jack. I found one with the window down. No alarm. I reached in, unlocked the door and hot-wired it. It had a full tank. Perfect. I parked in front of the eatery on the corner. Vinnie's ride was just a few feet ahead of me across the street. I knew the boys would come out first, then Vinnie. They'd check the car. They'd scan the surroundings, but they wouldn't see me. I'd take my shot, then keep on driving until I got to my bike. I'd dump the car, hop on my bike, and I'd be gone.

While I waited, I prepared the.357 Magnum I had brought with me, making sure it was fully loaded. Over the weeks, I'd cleaned and polished her relentlessly in anticipation. This was a good gun, powerful and in the hands of a competent marksman, which I was, accurate at long range. Two shots, one to the head and the other to the chest, would do the job.

I touched my forehead. It was wet. My hands were clammy but not shaking. Good. *I can't miss. I can't miss.* I took some deep breaths. Then I saw them, Vinnie's guys. They walked out and began their inspection. I started the engine, foot ready to release the brake and hit the gas. *Please. Let there be no one else in the way. If I hit an innocent, I'd be devastated.*

The door opened. I was breathing hard, in and out. There he was. I did a sharp turn of the wheel of the car and hit the gas. The car behind me leaned on his horn, which caused the three men to look up. Vinnie was in clear view. I had a shot. I held the wheel straight, put the gun out the window and squeezed off one, then two bullets. A look in my rearview told me Vinnie was down. I'd hit both marks. My attention on the road, I accelerated. I got the yellow light about to turn red and took the corner practically on two wheels. Then I slowed down. I did the block, shoved the gun into my pocket and abandoned the stolen car at the side of the road. I hurried into a back alley where I'd parked my bike. I got on and sped off in the other direction toward the highway.

I drove for about fifty miles, then stopped at one of those motels just outside the Texas border. I took a bottle out of my duffle bag and booked a room. I drank and tried to get some sleep. I was tired but stressed out. I turned on the ratty television and let the drone of voices send me into a trance. Eventually, between the booze and the television, I slept.

I didn't wake up until afternoon.

The moment I opened my eyes, I began to surf the channels for the news. I waited impatiently for the announcement while I wiped the gun clean of prints. I'd put it in a plastic bag, along with the gloves I'd worn, and get rid of them somewhere in Texas.

I took a long shower and thought about Colby touching me. It made me hard, and I jacked off under the spray. It helped to ease the tension. I was getting dressed in some clean clothes when I saw Vinnie's face on the TV.

Vinnie Carloota, well-known mafia kingpin, was gunned down last night after coming out of a mafia-owned restaurant in Little Rock, Arkansas. He died from two gunshot wounds on the way to hospital. Police have no immediate suspects. Carloota was rumored to have many enemies and has been associated with the criminal underground and suspected of racketeering, drug smuggling, money laundering, white slavery, and murder.

I let out a sigh of relief and took out my disposable cell phone.

"Diego. It's done."

"I saw the news. It's all over. Some are dancing in the street. The way I hear there won't be a lot of resources wasted on finding his killer. He was not a favorite of the police."

"I will be at the meeting spot tonight at ten. Get the body there, my money, and a vehicle."

"It won't be a Corvette." He laughed.

"Listen, I don't give a shit what it is, as long as it runs, it's not stolen, and it has a full tank of gas."

"I hear you. See you soon." He hung up.

I was back on the road. I could taste the freedom now. It was Colby and my mother who would suffer this next week, but as soon as the funeral was over, I'd call them. It needed to be convincing at that funeral. There could be no doubt I was dead.

I stopped in Texas to eat. I got rid of the gun and the gloves and ate a huge lunch. I was waiting for Badger at ten o'clock in a wooded area outside Dallas. I had an AK-47 with me just in case. I couldn't see him fucking me unless he really was a greedy bastard. I'd gotten rid of all his competition. He'd be raking it in without a lot risk. What more could he ask?

He came alone like I asked. And the car wasn't half bad, a small black Toyota with a sunroof. He got out. I tensed, my hand on the weapon.

"Diego?" He peered at me.

"Yeah."

"Man, I hardly recognized you with that beard. Relax man," he said. "No need for guns. You like the car?"

"It's not stolen?" I asked him, looking over at it.

He handed me the papers and the keys. "Nope. Bought it this morning at the car lot. Took it out of your million."

"Of course," I said. I checked the papers. "Great."

He took out an envelope and gave it to me. "The million minus nine grand for the automobile."

I took it, checked it. It was full of thousand-dollar bills and looked fine.

"Want to count it?"

I shook my head. "No."

"All untraceable."

"Good. And the new identification papers."

"Here you go. Social security card, passport, and birth certificate."

I checked the name. Diego Johnson. I made a face. "Johnson?"

He shrugged, then looked at my bike and whistled. "You sure you want to just leave her? She's incredible."

"You can have it. Tell Nuts it's your finder fee."

"Great. I love it. He might not let me."

"Where's the body?"

"Come on."

I followed him through the woods. "Under here." He brushed aside a bunch of leaves. There was a shallow grave with a body in it about my height. The body stunk to high heaven. It was burnt in some places and decayed in others.

"Shit." I covered my nose. "That's rank."

"You didn't come to a good end, my friend." Badger shook his head.

"I guess not." I realized that this guy could have been me.

"Give me your jacket. We'll leave it a few feet away. I'll mess it up a little, burn holes and shit."

"Who was he?"

"You don't need to know."

"Okay." I walked back through the woods to the road. "Wait a day, then call Nuts and tell him you found me."

"Are you sure about all this, Diego?" He stopped and looked at me. "I mean, hey it feels like my birthday, but you're giving up everything. You're the leader of the god-damned Banni for Christ's sakes." He was talking to me as one gang leader to another.

"Not anymore," I said. I took my jacket out of the duffle bag. With my knife, I cut down the middle of my palm and smeared some of my blood on it, then handed it to him.

He handled it with respect. I felt like stomping on the damned thing. "Good thinking," Badger said. "And I'm impressed with your hit on Vinnie. Wow. Care to tell me how you did it, so clean?"

"I don't want to talk about that or think about it anymore. I paid my debt." I looked at him. "We're square, right?"

He made the sign of the cross. "Rest in peace, Diego Champagne."

I took a T-shirt out of my bag and wrapped it around my hand to stop the bleeding. I opened the door to the car and threw the bag in. I gave Badger the disposable cell phone. "Get rid of it."

"You got it."

"Bye, Badger," I said. "Take care."

"I will." He grinned. "I don't have to worry about you now. That's a big load off, especially since I found out what a fucking crack-shot you are. You did that from a moving vehicle right?"

I didn't answer. I started the engine.

"Tell me one thing before you go."

I looked at him.

"What's your real angle here? I mean, what are you giving all this money and shit up for, Diego?"

"For love," I told him. "I'm doing this for love." I grinned and took my foot off the brake. As I drove away from Texas, I let out a shout. "Yes! Yes!"

I turned on the radio, and there was CCR. I was headed to Vermont, and I planned to take my time. When I got there, and the funeral was over, I'd call Colby and explain everything. I only hoped he loved me enough to forgive me.

CHAPTER FIVE

Colby

"You want to know all about me?" I asked the therapist. Shoot. Here she was, and here was I, forced to undergo anger management counseling. I still couldn't believe I was here. All because Garnet forgot her lunch box at home, and I'd interrupted her class to take it to her.

Well, that was only part of it. Truth be told, I'd punched Garnet's teacher in the face after he asked me, "Were you always this angry, or is it since you got custody of the kids?"

I'd done the unthinkable. I'd slugged him, rattled loose a few of his teeth, and shaken his bones. Personally, I thought Mr. Ken Waters looked much better after I'd finished with him than before, but the school board disagreed.

I stared at the therapist. I'd been forced to undergo eight weeks of one-on-one sessions with Pattianne Michaels. Three times a week. How aggravating. I'd had to hire extra staff to help at the bakery to cover my absences so I could be here.

This was the first day, and I didn't think I could hack it. But then I thought of my kids' miserable faces and took a deep breath.

"This hasn't been my best life," I said, a pathetic attempt at a joke.

Pattianne raised her eyebrows and smoothed down her skirt. An odd thing to do really, since it covered her knees and touched the top of her boots. It didn't seem to need her touch, but what did I know about fashion?

"How so?" she asked.

Oh, we are going to get along just great. I cued the mental sarcasm and eyed the wall clock. Her sessions were fifty-nine minutes long. Fifty-eight to go. Then I'd have to come back twice more this week. Any anger I had would be quadrupled by the time I was done.

"Nothing's gone right for me," I said. "Nothing. From the time I was a kid."

"You want to clarify?" She pushed her glasses up the bridge of her nose. She was an attractive woman in a Southern belle, hippie kind of way. Long brown hair with traces of purple tint through it. The flowing skirt and boots, and that Texas twang she had going on gave her an earth mother vibe that reminded me a bit of Cherise.

"My mother was a loon."

She looked at me.

"No. Seriously. She's in a state mental facility and has been for a long time. You can check. She clutches a headless doll she's named after me and beats it with alarming frequency. And, oh yes, she beat my baby sister to death. My father and his boyfriend, oh, and my sister June, too, helped conceal the evidence. Actually, I believe my mother kept Garnet in a cage and starved her and beat her to the point of death, and my sister killed her.

"She claims she ended her life by strangling her. Putting her out of her misery, I think is how she put it, until her fancy attorney told her to shut the fuck up and go for the insanity plea. My sister, Garnet Beauty's remains, were thrown in a water cooler in a forest in Alabama. When I went to visit the forensic pathologist at the university in Tuscaloosa several months ago, she told me that the reason I'd been unable to identify my sister from the artist's rendering was that she had suffered terribly since I'd last seen her.

"She said Garnet had suffered more than any little six-year-old girl should suffer. I am having a hard time living with that knowledge, Miss Pattianne. We had the funeral three months ago. My sister June and her husband are both in prison. I'm raising their kids with my boyfriend's mother, Cherise. She's a wonderful woman who's been undergoing cancer treatment through all of this.

"My father was an abusive asshole who was hell to live with my entire life. He was a sociopath, and proud of it. Then there's my father's boyfriend, Calvin. He got hit by a bus right in front of me and Cherise. My father died about a month ago, blaming me for Calvin's death when I had nothing to do with it.

"I got the kids into a nice house here in town, and some religious fucker turned our preacher's house into a blood-bath right after my baby sister's funeral. Shot up a bunch of people in it and kidnapped Garnet and Henry, who were visiting them. Oh, and to cap things off, the man I love more than anything, was murdered. They found his body five weeks ago. You may call it a persecution complex, but I call it one hell of a fucked-up life. And frankly, Pattianne, I see no good down the end of the road. If I didn't have those kids to take care of, I'd be gone. And that's the truth."

She stared at me. She didn't blink. Obviously, she knew all of this, she just wanted my version of the events. "Colby, it's a lot for anybody to deal with. I don't know what to feel sorrier for right now. But let's start with Diego. That's his name, isn't it?"

I couldn't speak. I couldn't hear his name let alone say it. It gutted me thinking of him in the past tense. I sat in my chair, opened my mouth to speak, but nothing but tears came out. Great racking sobs that hurt my whole body. Pattianne sat there and let me weep.

She handed me some tissues. "Are you okay?" she asked at last.

"No. I'm not okay. I can't believe he's gone. I cannot believe it. No matter what, no matter how many times I go to his grave, I just don't feel he's there."

"You're still at the first stage of grief," she said, her gaze full of sympathy. "That's understandable. Denial is a biggie. You will move from that to anger, guilt . . . but let's work on the denial."

I slouched now, feeling empty. That's what it was. I couldn't describe it any other way. My head kept telling me he was gone, but my heart wouldn't buy it. I hadn't seen his body because it was burned beyond recognition. The mob had gotten to him. It was Nuts and Duchesne who went to the morgue. Nuts had been a wreck for days afterward.

"You don't want to remember him that way, C," he said. "I wish I could bleach it from my fucking brain."

No, I did not want to remember that way. I wanted to remember his seductive smile. I wanted to remember how he looked when he looked at me. Like no other man existed.

Nobody had ever loved me like that, and I knew nobody would again.

Cherise and I cried a lot at night. We talked about Diego. We didn't name him. It was just *he* and *him*. She dreamed of him a lot and claimed to feel him close by.

One night she said that she felt he was alive. I thought so, too, and had been afraid I'd go mad if somebody didn't believe me. I was convinced he was out there. Somewhere. I know it sounds crazy, but I fully believed he'd escaped death.

Maybe it was because the coroner said his remains were so decayed that they couldn't tell for sure, but there was DNA evidence. They relied on that heavily, and I don't know why, but I refused to believe that body was his. I just felt I would know if he was really gone.

"You've been through a lot, and your stage of grief is understandable," Pattianne said. "Forgive me for trying to distill this terrible group of circumstances into manageable lumps, but I'd say the loss of your sister Garnet, your sister June, and Diego are the ones we need to deal with."

"I am not grieving June. I hate her."

Pattianne looked at me. I think she actually understood me, and that was even harder to take than her thinking I was some kind of angry, jumped-up fool.

"Of course you grieve her. You found each other again after being separated for years."

So, I was right. She knew everything about me.

"And from all accounts, you've supported her and her husband financially for several years. Then you found out she had a hand in your sister's murder."

"Literally," I muttered.

"And Judd. He was involved in a different homicide. He's been on the run hiding in plain sight as the saying goes. My God, Colby. Anybody would be devastated. I think you're doing incredibly well." She leaned toward me. She was sitting in a chair opposite me, awfully close actually. It was as though she didn't want me to escape her scrutiny.

Suddenly, I couldn't breathe.

"The hardest thing is letting go, Colby."

"Tell me about it." What I really wanted to say was, *What do you know about it?* but I didn't know her story. Maybe she'd experienced extensive loss, too.

"Guilt, anger, love, loss, betrayal . . . they all go together, unfortunately. Everyone and everything we love dies eventually. When a person we love leaves us, there is never enough time. We're never ready, even if there is a lingering illness. We are never really prepared for that final moment. We always want just one more day. One more hour. One more minute. We make bargains with God, or whatever deity we believe in. *Just let me hold him one more time. Just let me hear his voice. Let me see his smile."*

Boy, she had me nailed. She looked very emotional when she said, "You never got to say goodbye to Diego. You got no closure." She looked down at her notes and back up again. "Not that many of us ever do get closure. That's the most difficult thing to accept. Sometimes loss is loss. And for some of us, it's a tragic legacy."

I shut my eyes, not wanting to think about never being able to touch Diego again. He'd disappeared for ten long weeks, and then Cherise got a call from the police in Dallas, of all places. Neither of us had any idea what the hell he had been doing out there, but they said they'd uncovered his body in some woods near Mesquite.

They believed it was Diego. Well, neither Cherise nor I had believed it.

Rogan Duchesne had gone out there with Nuts. Man, those two were, um, well, nuts about each other. They flew to Dallas, and Rogan told me it had been devastating to see Diego like that. All burned and beat up. Whoever killed him had pulled all his teeth. They'd found some blood, and his discarded and burned jacket not too far from the body.

We'd had a funeral for him two weeks ago after the Southwestern Institute of Forensic Sciences released his body. He was cremated, his ashes buried right next to Garnet Beauty. She is the foundation of a Garnet Beauty peach tree. Cherise chose the same tree for him. I remember a lot of people showing up. I had no idea who many of them were. A few news crews. Damned human vultures, that's what they were. And one really weird, ultra-religious group protesting motorcycle gangs. But then, this particular group of freaks has been known to protest the funerals of innocent babies.

Any old cause in a storm, I guess.

I go visit Diego's grave sometimes, but I feel nothing. I

tried to speak to him one morning about how I feel, and then I got the call from Garnet's teacher about her lunch box. I went home, fetched it, and took it to school.

The teacher had threatened to give her a detention because I disrupted the class. I'd said a few choice things to him alone in the hallway. That was when he'd made the crack about my anger issues. I popped him one and wished I had my father's homicidal instincts.

But no, I don't. I paid the teacher's dental and chiropractic bills and agreed to these therapy sessions.

I stared out of Pattianne's tiny window at a tree and noticed a single shoe dangling from a branch. Some say dangling shoes from trees or telegraph poles are a signal for a gang meeting, but Duchesne claims this is an urban myth. I know it's not true about motorbike gangs. The knowledge that I was no longer in one swept over me. I didn't miss the life. I missed some of the guys. I still had Jerry, the only one apart from Diego who mattered.

Nuts was still in my life peripherally because of Duchesne. And Duchesne was having a tough time reconciling being involved with a gang member when he was on the other side of the law. I predicted a gang defection in Nuts' future.

The gang life reminded me of the crap we got involved in. The fighting. Bullets. The forensic pathologist found several in my man's body. Apart from his teeth, his fingers had been chopped off, and he'd been partially burned. He'd sustained a prolonged torture session and had been castrated prior to being torched alive.

God. Such cruelty in the world.

The Dallas police had held onto his jacket in case they got a break in his case. Not that there is an active one. They have nothing to go on. The mob wanted him dead, and somebody made sure he got that way.

My only consolation is that I love Henry and Garnet more than any other two people in the world, and I like to think of them being together. It has been hard to accept that my sweet little sister has been alone in Heaven all this time. But Diego, I am sure he's there, and I am certain he's with her.

If he's really dead, that is.

"Change is never easy," Pattianne said, her voice tender.

"Can I tell you something I've never told anyone? Not even his mother?"

She nodded.

"When I first found out he was gone, I mean, really gone, I kept seeing him everywhere. I'd be driving, and some guy crossing the road would look like him. I'd find myself following men I thought were him. An arm, a cheek, the back of a head." I blew out a sigh. "Is that weird?"

"No. Not at all. We fight to hold on. We fight to let go. We struggle to accept the unthinkable. Our hearts hold on. We see them everywhere. We believe they're still alive, because the world is not the same, it can never be the same without them."

I was sure she could read my very thoughts.

"I'm going to tell you something because I don't think you are a stupid man. I think you were provoked when that teacher spoke to you the way he did. You are a very protective father and uncle. I know some parents have written to the school supporting you. You need an outlet for your grief, Colby. You need someone who has no judgment and cannot turn around and sabotage you. That's all you've ever known. Betrayal and loss, and the moment you got some love, that was taken away from you. Violently, and without recourse."

There was so much truth to what she said. Diego and I had never had a chance. We'd always fought for every second we had together. And now I was being forced to let him go. Forever.

At his service, Anjohnette, that crazy long-lost aunt of mine, who hadn't even been invited, showed up and gave me a Christian memoriam card. She'd had some printed with a photo she got somewhere of Diego. It read, "Heaven is goodbye forever. I really must be going." I went berserk. Cherise wanted to read it, but I wouldn't let her see that card. She got hold of the damned thing, and I mean damned, and fell apart.

I had to take her home, and the doctor came and recommended a shot of Valium.

"Okay," I told him. "She doesn't need to go anywhere, give her a good dose."

"No," he said. "I mean the shot is for you."

I let him do it because it was better than feeling like hell. I woke up the next day, and I have been in torment ever since. Hell is a series of stages, and I've been in the mosh pit since Duchesne called me and said, "Colby, I wish I'd never had to tell you this, but it's him."

It's hard for me to function. I can't sleep or eat. I struggle with the kids and their various needs. Cherise and I are in agony. Sue-Ellen and Jerry are there for us, but Jerry is dealing with his own broken heart. He was in love with Calvin, and it was hard for him to accept that Calvin was an ass, even though the evidence was always there.

A week ago, we got drunk together, and he said, "Calvin helped your dad and June dispose of Garnet's body because he thought she died of natural causes. He thought he was protecting them and, also, he knew your mom was nuts and that any investigation into Garnet's death would send her over the edge."

He could see that it was a lame excuse at best. We were no comfort to each other, and the next day I got into the confrontation with Garnet's teacher.

I wound up getting arrested, and the judge, feeling pity

for me, ordered me to take anger management therapy. It was better than jail. I mean, poor Garnet and Henry really didn't need to have all their family members locked up in one facility or another.

"When you think about your time with Diego now, how does it feel?" Pattianne asked me.

I looked at her. "It seems almost like a dream. Everything feels like it never happened. I have nothing of him. A few photos I had on my cell phone are gone." I blinked back a tide of fresh tears.

She seemed happy with my response and leaned forward again. "That dreamlike quality is what helps us cope. It smoothes away the edges. Once you are past the denial stage, past the disbelief, you will start to have an acceptance, and then anger will set in. I know you've been displaying bursts of anger, but I would not classify you as an angry man. I would say you are a man in deep distress, who suffers depression, but that you feel you have no right to it."

I didn't know what to say. I thought she was right, but now I was afraid the first person who understood me apart from Cherise would tell me she couldn't help me because I wasn't angry enough.

"Can you remember the first moment you met him?"

I grinned. I couldn't help it.

"It's the first time I've seen you smile. Do you mind sharing that experience with me?"

Oh, God. I didn't think I could. It would tear me in two.

She waited then said, "What did you like about him?"

"His ass."

She looked at me, her head tilted to one side. "Really?"

"He was on a motorbike. We were heading to Austin, Texas for a big motorbike rally." My concentration faltered. I kept seeing him riding without a care in the world. His thighs hugged that chopper like it was his lover. I'd been in

Jerry's Corvette, and I coveted the rider. He coveted the bike.

"We liked each other," I said. "We stopped at some lights. I talked him into a quickie." I was embarrassed sharing this with a woman. We'd had hot sex, and then Jerry nearly died in a bar brawl.

"He saved my life," I blurted.

"By having a quickie with you?"

I shook my head. "No. Although, I guess he did. I didn't believe in anything until I met him." The realization hit me. It was the truth. Maybe that was what I was supposed to get from my relationship with him. The capacity to love another man. That and the Britten bike he'd treasured more than any of his other bikes. Cherise had given it to me because she said Diego would have wanted me to have it.

"I never slept with a guy more than once. Then I met him, and I knew I was in trouble." The words came out, and it hurt like hell, but it also felt good to talk about the love we shared and that could never, would never be.

"Colby, our time is up for now," she said after I'd bled all over her. "I'd like to help you. I think we can continue to work together. How would you feel about that?"

I took a deep breath. "I'd like that very much." It surprised me how much I needed to give voice to the times Diego and I spent together. The good and the bad. So far, I'd only told her the good. No need to talk about gang stuff.

She gave me a small, sweet smile. "I think you're a very good man, Colby Young. You never really had a childhood, and you've probably never had a decent relationship. You got a taste of it with Diego, and I'm glad you have Cherise, and that she has you. I hope I can help you move toward a happier state of life. By the way, I have a weekly group therapy session you should come to. I think you will enjoy it."

"Group therapy?" I balked at the concept.

"They're all gay men from different walks of life. Almost

all of you have had to live with your sexuality in secret."

"And you conduct these meetings?"

She nodded. "I guess you haven't figured out yet that I'm a transgender woman. I used to be a man, so it gives me a unique perspective on relationships and sexuality."

I was stumped. I didn't know what to say. She looked like a woman through and through to me.

"You're beautiful," I said.

She laughed, and for some reason it made me laugh, too.

"Thank you," she said.

"I'm gay, not ignorant. Do you date men or women?"

"I'm married to a woman."

Somehow, I didn't think landing me with the coolest chick I'd ever met had been on Ken Waters' agenda when he insisted I get anger management counseling.

"I'd like that," I said.

"Our first meeting is Thursday night, right after our individual session." She eyed the clock. "How do you feel?"

"Like the time flew. And a little less hopeless than I did before I came in here."

She beamed at me. "I hope you can hold onto that feeling tonight. I'm here if you need to talk. You can always call me, and if I'm unavailable, I'll get back to you promptly. I'll see you on Thursday."

We both stood, and she hugged me. She smelled of something familiar I couldn't identify, but it was a comforting smell.

As I left her office, I realized it was the same kind of soap Sue-Ellen sometimes used. Sue-Ellen would like this woman. A lot.

Garnet, Henry, and my dog Beauty were all lined up at the living room window waiting for me. Garnet's anxiety vanished the moment she saw me walking up to the door.

She squealed, Henry hollered, and Beauty barked. After they yanked open the front door, they threw themselves at me.

I smelled lasagna on the air and hugged and kissed them all.

"Beauty ate our dinner," Garnet informed me.

I cupped her sweet little face in my hands and kissed her. "She did? Is that why I smell tomato sauce?"

"Yeah!" Henry shouted up at me. Beauty kept leaping up trying to kiss my face. I held the children to me and hunkered down and gave my sweet, silly dog as much access to me as I could. She whined. Next thing I knew, she'd be pooping lasagna everywhere.

"Want to come for a walk?" I asked the kids.

"Yeah!" they screamed. It was a warm night, so I didn't make them put on sweaters, but I did send them inside for their shoes. Beauty was doing her gotta-go-now dance, and Cherise came out with her leash and a plastic bag.

"How did it go?"

"Not as bad as I thought."

"Good." She put her arms around my neck, and we hugged. Man, she was thin. Too thin. She started to cry like she always did these days.

"Call the bakery," I instructed. "Ask Gustavo to close up for me tonight."

"Are you sure?" she asked, her face glistening with tears as she pushed herself away from me.

"I'm sure."

She looked relieved. "I made a fresh lasagna. It's in the oven. You have twenty minutes."

The kids came crashing out. I leashed Beauty, then dipped down to take Henry on my shoulders and grabbed Garnet's hand with my free one. We walked down the street, and the children talked nonstop simultaneously about their days. A block down Beauty did her thing, and I cleaned up.

"Eww! Stinky!" the kids screamed. Henry hung onto my ears as I bent to scoop up after the dog.

"Your poop stinks too," I informed them.

"Not mine!" the kids shrieked.

"Oh, yes, you're very stinky!" I said, dropping the bag into somebody's garbage bin.

The kids laughed and laughed. I was surprised I got such a kick out of entertaining them so much. It didn't take much to make them happy, and it sort of tore at me that they had told me how much time they'd had on their own.

Garnet had told the social worker that she and Henry were often left alone locked in their bedroom. Their father would leave them for hours at a time. When he came home, he was frequently angry but never hit them.

"Daddy yelled a lot," Garnet told me. "I was afraid to tell Mommy that he left us alone. I would tell Henry to sleep. We never cried. We were good, Papa. I promise. We just closed our eyes and went to sleep." It reminded me of my own childhood; history would not repeat itself. June was always working, and Judd was supposed to take care of them. Now they were both gone, and Garnet and Henry were surrounded by adults who loved them.

Sue-Ellen loved to do Garnet's hair and put makeup on her. Henry got to play with Jerry's pet spiders. What Garnet loved, so did Henry, particularly Jerry's prized tarantulas . . . yuck! They always had either me or Cherise to run to. After the fiasco at Diego's funeral with my crazy aunt, she was not welcome in our lives. She'd called once or twice, but I always ended the calls quickly.

"I'm not crazy," she said the last time she called. She could have fooled me.

The kids and I covered the block in record time and made it home again. I'd had an odd sensation of being followed and told myself I was being foolish. Who would be following us? I looked over my shoulder as best I could with Henry sitting on it, but saw nobody. We walked up our front path and in the reflection of the living room window, I saw a man standing across the road watching us.

I turned, but the man was no longer there. We got inside the house, and I let Henry down to the floor.

"Anything wrong, Papa?" Garnet asked me. That's what she called me these days. Papa.

"Nothing, sweetheart, now wash your hands, you two. Dinner's almost ready."

The kids thundered down the hallway, Beauty right behind them. When the coast was clear, I nipped into the living room and dropped down, crawled to the window and peered out of the half-closed blinds.

Damn. There was somebody there. I stared at the guy. He looked skinny and sort of puffy-looking. He wore an ill-fitting suit and held an old-fashioned Fedora hat in his hands. He looked like he wanted to cross the road and come over then suddenly took off around the corner.

"Colby!"

I got up from the living room floor and shot through to the kitchen. The dog was eating her food in a stainless-steel bowl on the floor. She looked up giving me a glance that said, *I get to eat this, and you get all that delicious stuff.*

It didn't seem to matter that she'd been counter-surfing and scarfed down our dinner.

"You want some salad with that?" Cherise asked, handing me a huge portion of lasagna. I didn't, but I tried to be a good role model for the kids, so I said yes.

We all ate, sitting around the table, and Cherise suddenly put a hand to her neck. She swiveled around, then turned back again.

"What is it?" I asked wondering if the radiation treatments, the last of her procedures, were still causing her aches and pains.

"I think somebody's in our backyard," she said.

Shit. And I didn't have a gun. I'd been forced to give up everything on my attorney's instructions in case the police ever did a raid.

I bolted from my chair, the kids hot on my heels.

"Stay at the table!" I ordered. The kids retreated. "Beauty."

My faithful sidekick stood beside me as I opened the back door and saw to my astonishment the man in the bad suit.

"I didn't mean to scare y'all," he said, looking past me and a growling Beauty to Cherise.

"Oh, Cherise. Can you ever forgive me?" His face crumpled.

I turned to look at her, and she seemed astounded. "Maurice?"

"I'm sorry, Reesie. I shoulda stopped him. He came to see me and said he was gonna kill a man. I told him not to get killed, but he did. That fool got himself murdered!"

Cherise stared at him, her mouth hanging open. I knew who he was then. And I guess Beauty decided Maurice Champagne, Diego's dad, was no threat to her family because she stopped growling. She bounded out of the door and went over to him. She'd been forced to fight. He'd chosen to fight. Their mangled faces gazed at one another.

"Hello, girl," he said, and he looked up at Cherise. "You're still the most beautiful girl in the world, Reesie."

"Oh, you," she said. But I could tell she was moved.

"You should come in," she said.

Maurice looked at me. He held out a shaky hand to me.

Cherise put her arm around me and leaned on me for support. "You might as well know that Colby and the kids, they're my family now. Colby and Diego loved each other." Just saying his name reduced her to rubble.

I put my arms around her and comforted her.

"It's okay, Reesie." Maurice Champagne patted her arm ineffectually. I felt the kids joining us. I have no idea what he thought when he saw the kids wrapped around our knees.

"You like lasagna?" Garnet suddenly asked him.

"I'm a lasagna guy," Maurice said, nodding slowly.

"Me, too," said Henry. The kids moved between me and Cherise and drew him into the house.

"This is your grandpa," Cherise said. "He's Papa Diego's daddy."

"Ohh," Garnet said.

"Ohh," Henry echoed.

"Woof!" Beauty said and beat everyone back in the house.

I gave Maurice my chair, and I could tell it had been a while since he'd had a good meal.

"Why don't you take the kids to the bakery and pick us up some pie," Cherise suggested. "And maybe some beignets." She glanced at Maurice. "You still like beignets, Mo?"

"Haven't had any for a long time. You made the best I ever tasted."

A funny look came over her face. "Sit down, Colby. I'll make my own pie and beignets. And Maurice, what the hell have you done to your face?"

"You know," he said, looking embarrassed.

"I like your face," Henry said.

"I like your face too," Maurice said.

The kids laughed.

"You'd better eat your salad before the dog steals it," Garnet told Maurice, leaning into him. The kids showed no fear of his ruined face. Mind you, they'd never showed any fear of my dog either, even though half her face was a mess thanks to her life as a bait dog.

"She loves kale," Garnet announced.

93

"I'm kinda fond of kale myself," Maurice said. He ate like he didn't know where his next meal might come from.

Cherise busied herself with her mixing bowls and measuring cups. A flush had come to her cheeks. She kept looking back at Maurice as though she couldn't believe he was there.

"Am I dreaming?" she asked me at one point over the drone of the Mixmaster.

I remembered what Pattianne had said about the dreamlike state I'd been in being a way to cope. Whoever was up in the galaxy far, far away, had sent Cherise a little gift so that she, too, could get through these very rough days. I had no idea what Maurice Champagne's presence meant in our lives, but I felt it was a good thing for Cherise. And I would be there, willing to eliminate him if he presented any threat.

When I saw the way he interacted with the kids, I wondered what Diego would think. And then I thought, he probably already knows. He knows we're drowning, and he sent us a life raft.

I just wished to hell more than anything the life raft had been Diego himself. Nothing and nobody else would ever make me happy again.

As long as I lived.

Chapter Six

Diego

It's a strange feeling to watch your own funeral on television. Frankly, I was amazed that I warranted so much media coverage. My miserable claim to fame. I was actually amused at the adjectives they used to describe me . . . wise, charming, good-looking, and deadly. The news of my passing, a sound bite about the Banni of Louisiana, and the footage of the rather daunting Banni funeral ride, all were in hot competition with the murder of Vinnie Carloota. Finally, Vinnie's murder won out over my death, due to a primetime feature with the Italian mafia, and a special edition of the unsolved murders of notorious criminals. I didn't even make the list.

I watched the Banni funeral ride while reclining on a bed in a hotel room I'd rented in West Virginia. Nuts rode my bike out front. He wore my vest as a sign of respect and also as an indication that he was next in line for leader. They'd all get drunk after and have one hell of a party in my honor.

As I watched, my eyes filled with tears for some reason. I was in mourning, too. I guess I hadn't officially said goodbye yet. I'd made this decision because I knew this is what I wanted, but it didn't mean there wasn't a part of me that would find it hard to let go. I'd miss the open road. Just riding free. There'd always be a part of me who was there on that road, without a need to punch a clock or answer to anyone. What I wouldn't miss was the chaos and the violence. I really didn't like the fact that people would take one look at my jacket and either fear me or want to kill me. I did what I had to do for as long as I had to do it. But it was over now. The only one I wanted to answer to was Colby ... if he ever forgave me for faking my death and leaving him in the dark, that is.

It had been on my mind constantly. How in the hell was I going to break the news to Colby that I was alive? Did I send him an email? Did I call him up and say, *hi there, honey, ah ... Colby, it's me. Surprise. I'm not dead.*

God, I was in agony over that.

I wasn't far from New York City now. Actually, I'd be there late tomorrow. I'd stop for the night, then continue on to my final destination, which was Burlington, Vermont. It was the state's largest city and the perfect place to start a business. It was relatively gay-friendly as well being close to Quebec, Canada. I'd already scouted out some possible locations for a bike shop, emailing back and forth with a few people who were looking to rent or sell their commercial property. The real estate market wasn't bad either. I loved the old New England style houses. The schools seemed to be pretty good as well, but maybe we could afford to put them both in private school.

I was coming out of the shower when I saw Badger's face on the late-night news. I hurried over to turn up the volume. The announcer said that several members of the Texas Crushers had been arrested after police had raided a large-scale drug operation in Texas. There wasn't any mention of the mob or the Banni. I wasn't sure if this was the best news of my life or the worst. I sank down on the bed and contemplated the news. On the one hand, it meant that there would be no drug war between the Crushers and the Banni. My guys were safe. At least I didn't feel anymore as if I'd left them to the slaughter. But, Badger being arrested could mean that my entire world was about to fall apart.

Badger could try and cut a deal by telling the cops I was still alive and that I had iced Vinnie Carloota. Would he betray me to reduce his prison sentence? Damn fucking right. So the cops would have an all-points bulletin out for my ass. And if the mafia got wind of this, well they'd be hunting for me as well. They'd use Colby and the kids to get to me and that wouldn't do. Shit. Goddamn that stupid Badger. He was a frickin' idiot getting himself arrested. I wanted to kick his ass. I would have if he were in front of me.

So, now what? I get someone to kill Badger? He was the only one who could ruin all of this for me right now. No. This would never end. I needed to get out of the country. Canada. But that meant I'd need a whole new set of papers for me, Colby, the kids, and my mother.

I had no time to waste. I knew a guy, the best forger that ever lived, but I needed passport photos of Cherise, Colby and the kids. I'd have to contact him, tell him the truth now, so I could get what I needed to make us all Canadian citizens. I took a deep breath and pressed in his number. I knew he might not answer because my caller ID said unknown. And it was two in the morning there. Colby was probably sleeping.

Two rings and I heard his voice. He wasn't sleeping at all. Maybe he was like me. He couldn't sleep. I hesitated. I wanted to hear him say hello again.

"Who is this?" He paused. Then he said, "Diego. Please God, give me a miracle. Tell me it's you."

"Colby. It's me," I said.

There was complete silence on the other end of the line.

"Colby, don't hang up on me."

"Is this true?" His voice was shaking. "It is really you?"

"It's really me. Don't you know my voice?"

He just started sobbing.

I gripped the phone. My knees weren't going to hold me anymore. The tears rolled down my face. "I'm so sorry." I kept saying it over and over while he cried. "Please forgive me. Please baby, forgive me."

There was silence now. He'd stopped crying, but he didn't speak.

"Are you still there? Colby? Colby, I had no choice. I had to do it, and it had to look right, people had to believe it."

"You bastard," he said softly. "You fucking bastard."

"I deserve that. I love you so much."

"Fuck you," he replied but there no malice in his voice.

I smiled. "Will you? Fuck me?"

"You're a pervert. You should sleep on the damn sofa alone for the rest of your days."

"Yes. I know. But you won't let me sleep on the sofa." I smiled.

He actually laughed. "Damn you, Diego."

"Does that mean you forgive me?"

"No. It doesn't mean I forgive you. You have a hell of a lot of work to do."

"Okay." I closed my eyes a second. My soul was singing. Colby was actually going to forgive me. Maybe because he knew I'd done it all for us. "Well," I said, "if I have a lot to make up for, I can't do it from the sofa."

He groaned. "Oh God, I miss you so much. I dream about touching you."

"Me, too," I said.

There was the pause, then Colby asked me. "Did you kill Vinnie?"

"It doesn't matter."

"It matters to me. Did you?"

"I could have. The less you know, the better."

"They say it was the work of a professional hit man. I didn't think you were that good a shot."

"There you go, must have been a professional hit man then."

"Okay, don't tell me. You made some sort of deal, and that was the price. That's what I'm thinking."

"Stop thinking about that stuff."

"Fuck, Diego. Where in the hell are you? Are you all right?"

"No. I'm lost without you."

"Never mind the bullshit. Are you all right?"

I laughed. "It's not bullshit. Listen, I'm in one piece, but I feel disconnected not being with you. You want to call that bullshit, fine. It's true."

"I know. Me, too."

"Did you see the news?"

"No."

"I had a plan, but I need to change it."

"Okay, what plan?"

"One that involves you, me, the kids, and my mom all living a normal life far away from the shit."

"I know that's why you put me through this hell. You might have trusted me."

"I couldn't risk it. I'm sorry."

"But, Diego, I punched out a teacher."

My eyes widened. "You did what?"

"I . . . lost it and . . . Never mind. I'm in fucking anger management right now. Jesus, Goddamn it."

"And it sounds as if it's working well, too." I laughed.

"Don't be a smartass. Diego, damn it. I want to be with you. Where are you? I'll come to you now, tonight. I need to see you, to touch you."

"That's exactly what you can't do. Listen to me. You've got to go on acting the same as if I'm dead. Don't let anyone know I'm alive, not even my mother or the kids, okay?"

"Okay. But when can I see you?"

"I don't know. Soon, I promise. Listen, baby, you need to go to the passport office and get me a picture of you, Mom, and one of each kid."

"Why?"

"Just do it. I'll tell you more when I can."

"Where do I send it?"

"Get them in jpeg and send it to the email I have on this phone. Got a pen?"

"Yeah."

"Okay . . . it's JohnsonD256 at Hotmail."

"Got it. What's the Johnson D256."

"Johnson is my last name now. D for Diego and 256 is the number of the hotel room you were staying at the first time I fucked you."

"You remembered that?"

"I remember everything about you. And Colby, I love you so much. I'm sorry about all this. I know what I would feel if I ever lost you. I had no choice. Just send the pictures tomorrow, along with all the info on the kids' birthdays. Okay?"

"Okay."

"And don't punch out any more teachers."

"Diego, please, don't hang up just yet."

"I have to. This phone is dying."

"I know now I can't live without you. If it wasn't for these kids . . . well . . ."

"I knew the kids would keep you safe. And I promise I'll make myself immortal just for you."

"You better. Can we really be together now, normal . . . like a real family?"

"Yes. Normal, like a real family." I closed my eyes for a second.

"I have something I need to tell you."

"Do it fast." I checked the battery light.

"Your father is here with us."

"My . . . what?" My stomach turned into a knot.

"He's here. He said you met."

"Yeah. It was a truly inspiring meeting."

"He's come to be with your mom. The boxing has really left him with a lot of health problems. I couldn't turn him away."

"Do what you want. Just don't expect too much from me where he's concerned."

"Okay. Your mother has never accepted your death. She says you're still alive."

"Well, she was right. I guess mothers know." The phone died. "Shit." I threw it on the bed in frustration then lay down on it myself. "Colby, I miss you," I said aloud. A little while later, I was asleep.

The next day, I went to a phone booth and called the man everyone knew as Magic Ben. "Where are you?" I asked him.

"I'm not telling you shit until you tell me who you are," he said on the other end.

Magic Ben's reputation was stellar. The guy was discretion with a capital D. "It's Diego."

"Holy crap. I just saw your funeral. Very touching. Are you a ghost or something?"

"Yeah, or something. Listen, I need some work. I'll send you the pictures through email, along with the information. Can you do it?"

"I can do anything for a price."

"I need five Canadian passports and birth certificates, as well as social security numbers for three adults and two children."

"No problem. You know the routine. When you got everything together, send it to me. Scan the documents, and if you have any in computer format, send those along."

"I'll have them for you soon. What's the address?" I scribbled down the address he gave me. "Got it. I'll call you back."

"It's gonna cost you."

"How much we talking?"

"Thirty grand."

"Okay. Done."

Magic Ben hung up.

I got into the car and headed for New York City. I plugged the cell phone into the car charger, and when I stopped for coffee a couple of hours later, Colby had sent the picture along with a short note. *I miss you so much. I dream about holding you every night. I forgive you only because I have to. I love you way too much not to. Be careful. I want you in one piece. I have plans.*

I smiled and wrote back: *Got the pictures. Whoa to your pic, Colby. What a frown. Good thing you're so beautiful or that would be one scary photo. Is that how you looked just before you slugged the teacher? Just wondering. Kids are adorable though. Thanks for forgiving me. Trust me, baby. This is all because I love you so much. And as for your plans, of course I'll stay in one piece, but only for that reason. Horny as hell. My wrist is about worn out now. Love D.*

I made one stop at a passport place to get my new picture, then made a call to the magic man and forwarded the attachments, which seemed to take forever to transfer. And that's all it took. "When can I have them?" I asked.

"Three days. Canada has those chips in their passports now. Takes some creativity to do but it's manageable."

"Good. Do it," I said and hung up. Yet another hotel room, this time on Broadway. Broadway was great, but the novelty of staying in hotels was wearing off big time. I took a walk on the street but bypassed the liquor store. I bought a bottle of water instead. I'd promised myself no more booze once Colby and the kids were with me, and I was hoping it wouldn't be long now. So, water for me.

I drank the water and slept. My appetite had been way

off, and I'd dropped at least ten pounds. I'd eat breakfast somewhere in the morning.

I didn't call Colby, although I was tempted. I found it hard listening to his voice and being so far away. Also, I worried about any kind of communication. I woke up, watched the news. No more about the Crushers. I had to wonder. Had Badger already offered me up in exchange for a lighter sentence? I didn't want to know. I just wanted out of the country.

I left my room and found a breakfast place. It was expensive, and I left half of it on my plate. I walked around a little, then spotted my reflection in a store window. My hair was really long, and I looked scruffy. I decided to get a haircut in one of those places where they serve you fancy coffee. The woman at the hair salon said she was going to give me a haircut that was in style. "It will be shorter in the back, longer in the front."

I told her as long as it didn't make me look like a girl.

She laughed. "No chance of that."

When she got done with my hair and trimming the beard, I didn't look like the same guy. Two other hairdressers came over and raved over my haircut. I hardly recognized myself.

Then I went shopping and bought some new clothes, jeans, short, muscle shirts. Only when I turned around to check the jeans in the mirror, did I see it. That damned Banni tattoo that had hurt like hell going on. I hated the sight of it.

There were a lot of tattoo parlors in New York City. I stopped into one on impulse and asked the 64,000 dollar question. "Can I get rid of this tattoo?"

"Let me see it," the guy said. His face was tattooed with a large lizard. Good God.

I lifted the tank top and turned around.

"Wow." He touched my back. "That's incredible. That's art, man. Is that a gang tattoo?"

"Yeah." I put my shirt down and turned around.

He shook his head. "I can't do it here, but there is a place in Montreal. They use some kind of new laser treatment. Light passes through the skin and soaks up the ink. But man, it's beautiful. Why do you want to lose it?"

"Because that guy is dead," I told him.

The artist nodded. "Enough said."

"You got an address and number on that clinic?"

"Sure." He walked over and scribbled something down. "I refer a lot of people there. Mostly breakup cases. Never tattoo the name of your lover on you 'cause the new one doesn't like it."

"Actually." I smiled. "I was wondering if you might do one on my chest. There's no danger of me ever wanting it off, believe me."

"A name? You sure man?"

"Positive. Just put it above the left pec over the heart, in nice black letters. Colby. Just write the name Colby, C-O-L-B-Y."

"Come on over in the chair and let's get it done. I'll use some fancy letters. I'll show you the choices, and you tell me the font and which lettering you prefer."

I pointed to the lettering. "That's nice. Looks kind of Gothic. And font . . . well, not too large . . . about three inches wide."

"Cool." The artist let his gaze travel over me as I stripped off my shirt. "This Colby is one lucky guy."

I winked. "You bet he is."

Okay, so I flirted a bit with the tattoo guy. No harm in it. He flirted back, even invited me for a drink. I pointed to my new tattoo. "No can do."

He grinned. "Are you really faithful to just one guy, a man who looks like you?"

"Yeah." I nodded and smiled. "I love him."

"Like I said, he's a lucky guy."

I paid him and gave him a nice tip. He did a great job.

"Don't forget to apply the cream. But . . . hey for a guy who has had a tattoo like the one you have on your back, you need no advice. It must have hurt like hell."

Diego nodded. "More than you know, buddy. More than you know."

"Good luck in Montreal. They're great at that clinic."

"Thanks," I said. And Montreal was exactly where I was headed.

Two weeks later, I was in Montreal. I had all the Canadian documents in hand, and I'd gotten laser treatments on my back. Truthfully, my back hurt, but every time I looked at it and didn't see the tattoo, I forgot all about the pain. It was red though, and I had a hard time applying the antibiotic cream they gave me. I went back to the clinic every few days, and they did it for me. It was healing nicely, and they promised me it wouldn't end up looking all rough and bumpy. One day I got up, and the redness was gone, and so was the pain.

I left Montreal and drove through the Eastern Townships. I'd found a place to set up my bike shop around a lake in a beautiful little town called North Hatley. The guy wanted to sell his garage. He was ready to retire. There were houses for sale there as well, and I'd arranged to go and visit a few.

The Eastern Townships was beautiful. I would have loved riding my bike through all those turning hills and trees, but I stuck in the car.

I stopped at coffee place on the highway, got a large coffee, then went outside to the phone booth to call Colby. I had decided to get rid of the cell phone. There was a lot of information on it I didn't need to get out. Right now, it was at the bottom of the river.

It was seven in the evening where Colby was, only one hour behind the current time in Quebec. I munched on a hamburger as I waited for him to pick up the phone. I was really happy tonight. I felt like everything was finally coming together. We were so close now, I could taste it.

Colby answered right away. "Diego? Where have you been? I haven't heard a word."

"I had a lot of stuff to take care of." I smiled. "I didn't want to get distracted. Can you talk?"

"Hold on, I'll go in the other room."

I could hear the children in the background.

"Okay," Colby said. "Just talk. I need to hear your voice."

"Hello," I said. "I miss you."

"Oh, Diego. Me, too. Are you okay, baby?"

"Yeah."

"Did you see the news today yet?"

"No." I gripped the phone. "Why?"

"Badger bought it up in the joint. He was killed by some inmate. Retaliation probably."

"Really." I smiled. I know I shouldn't have. "He's dead?"

"Yeah."

"Shit," I said suddenly. "It just occurred to me ... I fuckin' did all this for nothing. He couldn't have had time to cop a deal ... or ... he could have ... I don't know. Did he say something or not? Doesn't matter. Maybe he didn't rat me out."

"What are you talking about?" Colby asked.

"Never mind. Sorry. Just thinking aloud. It was meant to be. Okay. This is what I want you to do, baby. Wrap up everything you need to do there. Buy five airline tickets for Montreal, Quebec. I'm going to send you your passports by courier today."

"Montreal, like Canada?"

"Yes. Say nothing to anyone."

"What am I going to tell your mother?"

"The truth. Do it gently but tell her."

"What about her house?"

"We'll deal with that later. Maybe she can sell it."

"Your father is here. I don't think your mother will go without him."

"Okay. Make sure his passport is in order. He has to travel separately if he comes. He's on vacation. That's all. Once he gets here, I'll make sure he has what he needs if he wants to stay with Mom."

"He's really a good man, Diego. There's a lot of him in you."

"Colby, don't expect too much from me where my father and I are concerned, okay?"

"Okay. I'm sorry. I won't. It should take me about a week. I'll be as fast and discreet as I can."

"Leave everything you don't need, except your personal belongings, or donate them. I'll call you back, and you can let me know when you're coming in. I'll be there at the airport to meet you."

"Why can't I have your number?"

"Not yet. I'll phone you." I checked my watch. "I need to hang up."

"Take care. And, Diego, please, don't let anything happen to you before I'm in your arms again."

"I won't. I promise." I'd be counting the days until Colby arrived. I couldn't wait to hold him, to kiss . . . and yes, to fuck him. I was looking forward to seeing my mother, too . . . and the kids . . . and well, as for good old Papa, not so much.

"Love you."

"Me, too," I said.

I heard the click. I guess I already knew there was a gun

pointed at my head before I turned around. I put the phone back on the hook, then froze.

"Don't do anything that is in your nature to do, Champagne."

I knew that voice. "You follow me here?"

"You only have one weakness, Diego. I tapped Colby's phone. I've been on your tail since New York City."

I closed my eyes. Shit.

"You'd risk everything for him, wouldn't you?"

"Yes," I said. I slowly turned around to face Duchesne. "If you're going to arrest me, then go ahead. Make your career."

"Step out of there," he said.

I left the phone booth.

"No sudden moves."

"You can pat me down. I'm not packing. I won't even fight. You want to send me to jail, go ahead. I'm finished. It's over."

He studied me for a minute. "Quite a makeover. You're really good-looking with the haircut and the trendy clothes, but I don't believe it will ever be over for you Diego. Once a Banni, always a Banni."

"Lift up my shirt."

"What?" He looked as if he was blushing. "Don't be ridiculous. I'm not going to do anything like that to you."

"Don't be stupid. Lift up the damn shirt and look at my back."

Duchesne looked baffled, but he pulled up my shirt and poked me with the gun. I turned around, and I heard him gasp. "My God." He let my shirt down. When I turned around again, he'd holstered his gun. "You mean it."

I nodded. "Listen, I have everything I've ever wanted now. I have a legitimate way to make money, a man I love, two kids, and my mom. There's nothing more I need. I just want a chance, Duchesne. I'm asking, no I'm begging you, give me a chance." I met his gaze. My throat constricted.

Duchesne slowly nodded. He turned his back. "I never saw you. I was . . . mistaken."

"Does anyone else know about . . ."

"I'll tell them I was wrong. That Colby has a new lover. It's not you he was talking to. I'll get rid of the tapes."

"Did Badger rat me out when he was arrested?"

"No. You killed Vinnie. You don't need to agree but just sayin.' No big tragedy. You did society a favor on that one."

"Thank you, man."

"Nuts thinks you're dead. He's really torn up."

"Guess you'll need to comfort him then."

I heard him chuckle as I walked away. "Guess so," he said.

I got into my car and drove away. He didn't follow. I didn't begin to breathe normally until I got to North Hatley.

The guy at the garage was an old Scotsman named Angus McCarthy. He showed me his garage, and it was perfect. We had a great talk about when he was in the war and used to fix tanks. I told him about the custom bikes I made, and he was intrigued. He invited me for supper. I ate some good stew with homemade bread. The guy was a bachelor, and he knew how to cook.

After supper, he brought out a bottle of Scotch whiskey, and I couldn't say no. We drank and talked until two in the morning. I was falling asleep in the chair. This is the type of relationship I'd missed in my life growing up, just sitting around talking with an older man . . . a father figure. It was nice.

When Angus noticed that my eyes were closing, he offered me a place over the garage to stay. There was a little two-bedroom apartment. I slept in one room and Angus in the other. It was clean and quiet, and I slept like a baby. The appointment at the notary was day after tomorrow, and then the garage would be mine. I told Angus he could stay in the apartment up over the garage for nothing. He was happy about that and offered to give me a hand with the bikes.

"That would be great," I said. I knew he was afraid not to feel useful anymore.

That night as we were talking, Angus told me about a house in town that was for sale. "It's not listed. You can get it for a song. It's a beautiful old New England house with five bedrooms and a big porch outside. There is lots of land. The kids could even have a horse if they wanted. It's a five-minute walk to the school."

"Sounds great," I said.

Angus offered to take me to see it the next day. "I'm good friends with the owner," he said. "We even dated a few times after her husband, Percy, died."

"And?" I grinned at him.

"Oh, I'm far too set in my ways," he said. "She wouldn't have me. Anyway, she'll be happy that you and your wife have kids. She raised her whole family in that house."

"Ah, Angus," I said. "Colby isn't my wife. Colby is a guy."

Angus's eyes widened. "Oh . . . you're one of those fellas."

"Yes." I nodded. "Colby and I are raising his niece and nephew. The parents weren't up to parenting." I left out the criminal part. "They've had a rough time of it."

"Well then." Angus patted my bicep as he drove. "We need to give them a good place to live."

I nodded with a smile.

"My goodness, fella," he said, patting my bicep again. "No one would want to go messing with you. You got muscles hard as rock. Know anything about chickens, Diego?"

"Chickens?" My eyes widened. "Only the kind you eat deep fried."

"You can raise chickens if you want."

"I'm not sure if I'm ready for chickens," I told him.

He chuckled. "A garden at least?"

"That I can do."

Angus's friend and the owner of the house in question was a nice elderly lady called Mrs. Grey. She was waiting for us at the house.

I fell in love with it the moment I saw it. It was a sweeping, two-story house with green shutters and a veranda that went all the way round.

"This is Mr. Johnson," Angus told Mrs. Grey. "He's a nice fella. Going to start a bike shop in my garage."

I grinned when Mrs. Grey said, "I like bicycles."

"Motorbikes," I said.

"Oh." She appeared to shudder. "Those things. They're noisy."

I nodded. "They can be."

"I had to give up this house and go live with my daughter a year ago," she said. "The place has been empty. Shouldn't be empty, this house." She opened the door with her key. "I raised six kids here, young man."

"Six? That's a lot of kids."

She nodded. "Yes, it is. Come and see her." She waved her hand around as we stepped into the living room. "She's a beauty," the woman said.

Hardwood everywhere: the floors, the staircase, and the beams. There was a fireplace in the living room and another in the master bedroom. I could see Colby and me lying together on the bed on a cold winter's night, fireplace blazing. It was spacious, the rooms were large, but it needed a lot of work. We'd need to redo the kitchen and both bathrooms to bring them up to date. And the wiring would all have to be changed. It was heated by oil and wood. I preferred electricity. But with the price she wanted, we could do all these things.

"Are you handy?" she asked, pointing to a broken knob on one of the kitchen cupboards. "Can you fix that?"

She was really sweet, this old woman, and I didn't want to tell her that the knob on the cupboard was the least of my worries.

"I think I could manage it." I grinned at her. "I love the house." I hoped Colby liked it. I wouldn't buy it unless he gave his approval.

"I need to talk to my partner," I told her. "I don't want to buy it until he sees it."

"No problem. Bring her round. Women are fussy about kitchens."

"Him," I corrected.

The elderly woman just stared at me.

"He's not here yet. I'll send some pictures."

She nodded. "I can leave the key with you. Come back when you like."

I thanked her. Angus dropped me off in town, and I was told I'd have to go to the nearest city, which was Magog, to buy a cell phone and set up a contract. It was less than a half hour drive.

Two hours later, I was back at the house. I took some pictures with my new phone and sent them to Colby with this heading: *What do you think?*

I went back to the garage to talk with Angus, then invited him to have supper with me in the local diner. We were waiting for our meal when I got an email from Colby. *Where is this place? It's beautiful.*

I smiled, excused myself to Angus, who was chatting with the people at the next table anyway and walked outside. I dialed Colby's number.

He answered right away. "Oh my God," he said. "Finally."

"You're out of breath. You been doing the nasty with

some hot stud?" I teased.

"No." He laughed. "I couldn't find my phone. I think the kids hid it from me. And you're the only hot stud I want to do nasty stuff with. What is that place?"

"It's our new house, but only if you like it."

"I love it. Tell me about it."

"Five bedrooms, big rooms, and lots of land, kids can walk to school. It's beautiful here, quiet. I'm ten minutes from the bike shop. We will need to do some renovation, but the structure is sound."

"Buy it."

I laughed. "Okay, boss."

"I'm glad you phoned. I got all the papers. They look great. Our reservations are for next Saturday. We'll be in at three in the afternoon if the plane's on time."

"I'll be there to meet you. I'll wait by the luggage thing. So, did you tell my mother I'm okay?"

"Yes."

"And how did she take it?"

"Amazingly well. She said she'd never doubted it. She believes you to be invincible, I think."

I laughed. "Good. I *am* invincible."

"Both parents are really relieved."

"Colby. I don't have parents. I have a mother. Don't do that."

"I'm sorry. You're pissed at me now."

"No. I love you. Just don't try to play family therapist."

"Okay. I have your phone number now. Can I call you?"

I laughed. "Bet you say that to all the boys."

"Seriously? No. Diego, I need to tell you something. I'm so happy, I'm scared."

"About?"

"About something going wrong. It's not right to be this happy. The only thing that would make me happier is to have you by my side right now, preferably naked and in my bed."

I grinned. "Love the way you think."

"You know what the kids said when I told them we were going to be a family?"

"No."

"Henry said, I hope this means you guys aren't going to be kissing all over the place and Garnet gave me the thumbs-up and said, "Uncle, you scored. Diego is cute."

I burst out laughing. I hoped he still thought so. I looked different — thinner, shorter hair, no beard, just a nice shadow, which I'd worked on perfecting. I wanted to look nice for him. I was going to wear these really nice jeans, with a khaki muscle shirt. "We're going to have to watch her when she's in her teens."

"You bet," Colby said.

"You have my number now. Don't wear it out. It looks desperate when you call a guy too often for a date you know."

"Yeah, right. Fuck off," he said, laughing. "You're going to pay for that one."

"Hope so. Punish me, baby. I love you, but I gotta go. My dinner is here. I'm having dinner with Angus."

"Who's Angus?"

"See you Saturday." I grinned. Let him worry about Angus.

"So that was the missus or . . . ah . . . the mister?" Angus eyed me when I came back to the table and put the phone away.

I smiled. "That was him."

"Taste the spaghetti, it's great."

I lifted a forkful. I was suddenly really hungry. "Mmm."

"So how does it work, two guys and all?" he asked.

"In what sense?" I was teasing him.

114

He kinda blushed, then threw his napkin at me. "Diego, really. I meant who cooks and cleans?"

"We share everything." I had a sneaking suspicion that Angus might have had some confusion about his sexuality when he was younger and that's why he stayed alone. He seemed very curious about Colby and me. "We're partners," I told him.

"That's the way then." He nodded. He lifted his glass of Coke. "Welcome to North Hatley."

"Thanks." I chinked my glass of water.

"So, when does the family arrive?" He bit off a piece of his garlic bread and met my gaze.

"Saturday," I said, and really, I couldn't wait.

CHAPTER SEVEN

Colby

It was a little before nine A.M., and I was tense. I'd had an unpleasant conversation with Maurice that I couldn't quite shake, and now, somebody was following me.

I turned a couple of times as I walked along Magazine Street toward the bakery I was in the process of selling. I couldn't see anyone when I looked over my shoulder, or, when I checked my reflection in the windows of the stores I passed. But I knew, just knew I had a tail.

Don't act nervous. *Look natural. Natural? What's natural about any of this!*

Nothing can go wrong now. The kids and I are almost out of here. Just a few more days.

I steeled myself to face the road and kept walking ahead. I could already smell the wonderful raspberry jam-laced king cakes on the air. The holidays were coming, and the lines outside the bakery never seemed to abate these days. I was selling at a good time. We were making good money. I'd socked a lot of it away, and liquidated my assets, including the pool hall that had been my bread and butter for years. I loved Diego and wanted to be with him but uprooting me and the kids was harder than I had first thought it would be.

I'd been involved in the bakery as an investor for years. Now, as the owner, I'd learned all my sister's secret recipes. I'd taken classes and worked with the staff June Gold had hired. Today, I could bake just about anything. I'd worked hard to reinvent myself.

Now I had to do it all over again.

Maybe I could open up a new bakery in North Hatley. The town had a small population, but everyone liked bread, right?

It was difficult not to turn around and look over my shoulder once more. I couldn't imagine who'd be following me. Or why. I was out of the gang. My father was dead, and I couldn't think of one person who would carry out a death-bed wish on his behalf.

Somehow though, the scene played out in my mind. Cledus shackled and cuffed to his hospital bed, begging some crazed fan, some inmate who maybe knew him way back when as the fearsome mofo he'd once been.

"Kill him! Kill Colby for me! Avenge me!" I imagined my father imploring.

The hairs on the back of my neck began to prickle. Could it have played out that way? Man, I had to stop watching *The First 48*. That TV show had done my head in when I'd watched it the previous night. It had disturbed Maurice as well. The reality show, which follows homicide detectives in the first two days of an investigation, had focused on a twen-ty-eight-year-old man murdered outside his grandma's house, right here in New Orleans. The case had garnered a lot of attention, but now, it transpired, it was the guy's wife who did it.

Yep, she'd set him up in an elaborate murder-for-hire scheme. It also seemed she may have had some involvement in her first husband's death, too. As long as I live, I'll never forget the lead investigator's words.

"Her reign of terror is over," he said. "She's off the streets."

"Dang, Colby," Maurice said as we sat on the sofa watch-ing the police finally track her down.

"You know why we're here?" the lead investigator asked her.

"Yes," she said, in a small, thin voice, clutching her newborn baby to her. "I called my mom, she's on her way."

"She's so cold," I said, as she handed off her child into her mother's arms, then climbed into the back of a police car, her facial expression one of chilly composure.

Maurice and I took in her mother's hysteria, the mounting horror as she realized her daughter had been involved in murder. "What did you do?" she kept shrieking. "What did you do?"

As the show's credits rolled, Maurice let out a ragged sigh. "I was involved with a chick like that once. Hard to get away from the crazies."

"How did you get away from her?" I'd asked.

"I didn't." He shook his head, palming his face.

Okey-dokey then. I don't think I want to know what that means.

We hadn't discussed it further, until this morning, when, after what he said was a sleepless night, he cornered me in the kitchen.

"Son," he said, his banged-up face looking worse than usual. "We need to talk."

My mind still reeled, recalling his words. Over a cup of Cherise's best chicory coffee, he told me everything. I didn't want to know any of it, but I had to know.

It had shocked me to learn that Maurice had just run out on the woman who had two babies by him and that she now knew where he was. She'd had him traced from Alabama, where he'd been living, on and off, with her. Turns out she's twenty-four, which is awfully young.

"She met me at the gym. Beats me up sometimes," he said, giving me a snaggle-toothed smile. "And sometimes, I deserve it."

Yeah, I bet you do, old man. I didn't want to hear any of it. Not a word. I thanked God it had all come out now and not when we were at the airport trying to fly out of the country. Having Maurice arrested for nonpayment of child support would land him in the slammer and draw attention to us. That would be a disaster when I'd so carefully planted a story to all and sundry that we were relocating to Australia.

"How did she find you?" I'd asked Maurice, surprised at how calmly I took the news.

He looked uneasy when he said, "She hired a private investigator. He followed me." He let the significance of all this settle over me before saying, "Cherise told me about Diego. I want more than anything to come with y'all. I wanna start a new life and be the daddy and granddaddy you, and Diego and those sweet li'l chillun deserve." His face crumpled. "But I got two kids wit' dat girl, and I can't stand the thought of runnin' out on 'em the way I did on Diego."

And so he was going to run out, again, on the two people who were used to it. *Fuck you, old man*, I wanted to tell him.

I didn't know what to say as he rambled about the crazy chick he'd fathered two kids with. He seemed genuinely frightened of her. "Beautiful," he said, "but deranged."

But you keep going back to her. I wanted to yell at him and punch him. I wished in that moment that I had some of my father's more dominant genes and could slug the guy into oblivion. Diego didn't want Maurice in Canada, but I had no idea how Cherise would take these latest developments. She'd seemed so happy lately. She had stood in the living room one evening describing her philosophy on improbability of ever finding romance again as, "Standing in the fire and looking for love. Who knew it was right there all the time?"

I swallowed hard. I kept thinking about that poor guy on *The First 48*, gunned down outside his grandma's house. She'd seen it all. She would never forget that day. And poor Cherise. She'd had to give up Maurice before. Could she handle it again?

Oh, man. What if Maurice's girlfriend is following me?

Fool! Why would she follow you?

We couldn't take the risk of letting Maurice accompany us to Canada. Lord, I hoped Cherise wouldn't make a stink about it. I'd worked hard to nurture her body, mind, and spirit now that she'd completed all her cancer treatments. I was shocked that she still had to take it easy. Cancer hadn't finished with her yet. Her doctors had warned her not to spend time outside in the sun. Her skin was in a fragile state from all the chemo and radiation. She and Maurice had discussed driving to Canada. A second honeymoon, they'd tittered.

But that couldn't happen, especially now. She'd have to fly with me and the kids, which was fine, except that we were now making plans to ship all our household items, plus a few irreplaceable custom-built motorbikes—including Diego's Britten—to our new home.

She was back at the house, packing. How would she take the news about Maurice? I'd made him promise not to say anything to her until I could be there in case she needed me. I knew exactly how she would cope with it.

Not well. She still loves that old coot.

My mental checklist kept growing. We still had so much to do, and it hadn't been easy keeping secrets from everybody around us. My mounting anxiety got the better of me. I had to get off the street. Whoever was following me could wreck my business sale. As I approached Louisiana, I contemplated ducking into Dat Dog, a dilapidated-looking hot dog joint, but chose the New Orleans Music Exchange next to it, right on the corner. I think it was the bars on all the windows that made me feel I'd be a smidgen safer in there.

A young couple pushing a baby buggy tried walking around me. Perfect. I eased off to the left, then sprinted into the music store. The windows were grimy, and the place was packed with guitars, amplifiers, and stacks of opened cases featuring everything from trombones to antique piccolos. I dropped down to the floor and squinted out of the window over the edge of a cello case and watched the sidewalk.

I was being followed.

But I was in shock to see that it was my mad aunt, Anjohnette, doing such a poor job of tailing me. What the heck was that crazy woman up to? I hadn't seen her since she'd crashed Diego's funeral. I began grinding my teeth, a nervous habit I'd developed since Diego's 'death.'

Boy, was he gonna pay with his ass for putting me through this shit.

I waited until she blew past me, ran back, then went the other way again. Who was it that said, "Confusion to our enemies?"

She glanced inside the music store just as an associate asked me, "Can I help you?"

Anjohnette didn't see me low to the ground there and kept moving.

I shook my head, smiled at the associate, waited another minute, pretending to examine the highly polished English horn nestled in grey velvet in a black leather carrying case. Young Henry had shown interest in learning an instrument.

No. Not a horn. I closed my eyes. The kids made enough noise as it was.

I ducked out of the shop and darted down Louisiana Street, then went a couple of blocks over and doubled back to the bakery.

The new owner was waiting for me. He wore a suit, and the guy he'd brought with him looked like some kind of Mafioso with his black-on-black getup and his mirrored shades. We got down to business in the back office. They'd accepted all my terms. They didn't even need to keep me on temporarily to show the new owner the ropes.

"I'm buying this business for my sister," the buyer said.

I wanted to tell him he was a fool. It took everything in me not to say, *Well, I hope she appreciates it. And I hope she isn't a homicidal maniac.*

"I'll have my attorney look over the contracts one more time," I said. "But it looks pretty good to me. We'll be in touch very soon."

"No problem. You're heading out to Australia next week, aren't you?" the new owner asked.

"Yes, I am."

"Best of luck to you."

"And to you." I shook his extended hand and picked up the contract copies. I left via the back door. I hate goodbyes, and I knew I wouldn't be back here. That was hard. I'd enjoyed my time here.

What was it that Anjohnette's funeral card for Diego had read? *Heaven is goodbye forever. I really must be going.*

This was a sort of death, leaving behind everything I knew. I'd Googled North Hatley, and it looked beautiful. A fresh start would do us all good. And Diego was there.

I had one more errand to run; picking up the kids' school records. I needed those for their enrollment in Canada. We'd figure out something when I got there, even if it meant homeschooling for now. At the door of the principal's office, my cell phone rang.

A text from Cherise: *911. Don't come home.*

What the hell was that supposed to mean? Of course, I high-tailed it back there and almost fell over when I tore into the living room, imagining all kinds of murder and mayhem, only to see a group of people sitting around, apparently waiting for me. Cherise and Maurice looked up at me. She looked apologetic. He looked a little . . . disgusted.

I looked around, stunned to see Anjohnette, my attorney,

my therapist, a couple of the Banni, and even, God help me, Rogan Duchesne.

"What the hell's going on?" I blurted.

"This is an intervention," Pattianne Michaels said.

"An intervention?" I almost laughed. "For me?"

"We're worried about you," she said. "Are you willing to surrender yourself voluntarily to a seventy-two-hour hold today?"

I gaped at her. I could feel Cherise's gaze burning into my flesh. "A seventy-two-hour hold? Are you kidding?"

"You are exhibiting signs that have all of your friends and family members concerned. Are you planning to commit suicide?" she asked.

I stared at her. This was crazy. No. Wait. She was insinuating I was the crazy one.

"What's going on, Pattianne? I've done everything you asked me to do. I've completed all my counseling. I've even done the wraparound sessions you recommended."

"Take a seat, Colby." She patted an upright chair beside her. I took it, my anxiety ratcheting up a few more notches.

What the hell gave her the idea I was planning to take my own life?

She glanced down at her clipboard. "You've been getting rid of things that are otherwise valuable to you. You've sold your businesses. You seem extraordinarily happy for someone who's been in grief counseling, and . . ." She held up her hand. "You no longer seem angry."

Everybody watched me. I couldn't believe this was happening. Diego would suffer for this. If anyone would die, it would be him. With me fucking him to death.

"I have no desire to end my life," I told her.

One day, I'll look back on this and laugh. I had to avert my gaze from Cherise. I was afraid we'd both lose it right here and now. The last thing I needed was to wind up in the nut house.

"You have a history of insanity in your family," Pattianne said.

I could have strangled her.

I sighed. "It's skipped my generation. Look, you're a fantastic therapist. I've confronted my grief and my anger, and I don't feel so bad anymore."

Pattianne's mulish expression wavered, her eyes darting from side to side. "Really?"

"Really," I said. Boy, and she thought I needed therapy. I turned to my attorney. "Steve, and what are you doing here?"

He had the grace to look embarrassed. "Pattianne said she was worried about you." As he spoke, I could hear Pattianne whispering to Cherise.

"He's going to ask Colby a few questions, and if he doesn't respond in an appropriate manner, then I'm recommending an immediate involuntary hold."

Steve glanced at me, and his cheeks flamed. "Um, ah, so, what's the weather like on Saturn?" he asked.

"Say, what?" I stared at him. He repeated the question.

"I have no idea what the weather is like there," I said, trying to keep the stiffness out of my tone. "Do you?"

Cherise and Maurice laughed. Pattianne silenced them with a look.

"What other questions you got there, Steve?" I pointed to the piece of paper in his hand.

"I'm sorry, Colby." His cheeks had flushed a crimson shade that made me think he had blood-pressure problems.

"Go on. I'm keen to hear them."

He shrugged. "Well, who's the president of the United States?"

"Barack Obama. Does that response really determine my sanity?"

"What year are we in?"

"Oh for corn's sake —"

"Answer the question!" Pattianne snapped.

"Twenty sixteen." I was afraid to smile at her. She was becoming unglued.

"You were a wreck!" she suddenly shouted. "You were depressed and angry."

"And?" I asked, keeping my voice low. "Why are you doing this? Spoiling all the good work we've done together."

She swiveled her gaze toward my mad aunt.

"Don't look at me," Anjohnette asked. "He's crazy. Takes right after his mama. Everybody knows it's hot on Saturn." She nodded her head vehemently.

Steve leaned closer to me. "I knew that was the correct answer." He gave me a conspiratorial wink.

I couldn't wait until we got rid of everybody. Cherise was a lot more sociable than I. She said goodbye to everyone. Maurice went off to the barber, or so he said, and Cherise walked outside with Pattianne, who kept trying to explain her silly motives, and Anjohnette went off to some Bible study group. Nobody suggested she needed an intervention. I would have staged one if I gave half a shit about the woman.

Outside near the footpath, Pattianne bent Cherise's ear. I wasn't worried about Cherise's loyalty.

Steve, the attorney, picked up the contract copies to check over, apologizing for his part in "Saturn-gate." He swallowed a couple of pills with a glass of water. "That was a bad business. Sorry, Colby."

"You'd better not be charging me for the hour you were here trying to prove I'm crackers, Steve."

"No, no. I'm not. Of course not. I'm really sorry, Colby. That was so embarrassing."

For me, and for him. His skin color was still a dangerous tone.

"You okay?" I asked.

"Yeah. My fault. I got a new girlfriend, and I took Viagra last night. Really doesn't mesh with heart conditions."

Yow, dude. Too much information!

"Are you okay?" he asked, gulping at his water.

"To be honest, I felt like I was in the middle of my own version of *Mr. Deeds Goes to Town*. You know, the one where his neighbors say he's pixilated. I think everybody in this house today is crackers if you ask me."

He looked at me. "I might charge you for my time here after all."

I shook my head.

"I'll get back to you," he said and walked off down the front path just as Cherise returned.

"We need to get the kids from school," she said. She looked exhausted, and I was certain she knew about Maurice's crazy girlfriend. I was angry he hadn't waited to tell her. Cherise didn't say a word. She just started to cry. I took her into my arms and held her.

"How soon can we leave?" she asked when her tears finally subsided.

"As soon as we like."

She pushed herself away from me. "I'd like to go in a couple of days. Everything's being picked up tomorrow. Did you get the school reports?"

"Naw. Didn't get a chance. I got to the school, then you sent me that weird text."

"I tried to warn you, sweetheart." She dabbed at her eyes. "There's something you should know."

Man, could I take much more drama today? "Tell me," I said.

"I don't want Maurice to know the address where we're

going. I want no further communication with him once we've gone."

"Understood." That relieved my mind. I'd worried she'd fight to take him with us. She paused. "He's going to Little Rock, Arkansas, tomorrow for cataract surgery. He has to go there. Something to do with his health insurance from his last fight. It's only good for the city he fought in." She paused again. "He's planning on coming back and flying to Canada with us. I can't have him with his baby mama chasing after him all the way up there."

I couldn't have agreed more. I felt a huge wave of release from all the stress wash over me. We'd have to leave sooner than planned. I didn't care. Frankly, the sooner, the better.

We walked down to the school with Beauty and picked up the kids, returning home hand-in-hand with them.

"When are we moving?" Garnet asked me.

"Soon," I said. I didn't want to get too specific with Maurice still in the house.

"Good," she said. "I don't like it here, anymore."

"You don't? Why not?"

She seemed to consider the question. "I don't know. It doesn't feel like home anymore."

I knew exactly how she felt.

Sue-Ellen and Jerry came over for an early dinner. They knew we were moving to Canada and not Australia. They were already talking about moving to Canada, too. They mentioned it but couldn't say much once Maurice returned.

Cherise and I stared at his head. He'd been gone for hours, and he didn't look like he'd had a haircut.

As soon as he went to the bathroom, Cherise grabbed my arm. "Please make arrangements for us to leave tomorrow night."

127

We flew out of New Orleans to Toronto the following evening on a Delta flight that took off at five-fifty in the evening. I still have no idea how we pulled it off, but we had everything organized and ready to ship in record time once Maurice left for Little Rock in the morning.

He swore undying love and devotion to Cherise, who acted like she believed him.

"He stunk of her perfume," she said to me as the shipping company came to take away our belongings a few minutes after Maurice's cab took him to the airport. "He gotta be crazy, Colby. I lost my sense of taste, not my sense of smell with the chemo. And I sure as hell didn't lose my mind."

She banged a few boxes of books around. I hoped it made her feel better. The only things we'd be flying with were our suitcases, and Beauty, who had her own travel papers and passport. Just like a person.

The kids were excited, but the dog got anxious every time things left the house. Since her humans were still standing with her, though, Beauty stayed cool. In the early afternoon, Sue-Ellen and Jerry took us to the airport in two vehicles. Sue-Ellen may be a tough bird, but I was told that she wept the whole way.

I would miss her, too, but I knew she and Jerry would at least come up for a visit. They could have a good look around North Hatley and see if they liked it. There wasn't a single other person I cared to stay in touch with, but I would miss her and Spider. Oh, and maybe I'd miss Duchesne. He'd been a constant force in my life. Maybe I'd drop him a postcard one of these days, but it would be weird.

Beauty hated being in her crate in the cargo hold of Jerry's SUV. She whined a bit but calmed down again when she realized she was coming with us to the airport. Either that dog is psychic, or she understood the things we said to her. I had a pang of anxiety when she was wheeled away by the quarantine people. All her paperwork was in order. We'd be able to collect her in Toronto.

"She'll be fine," Jerry assured me.

I nodded, but I wasn't so sure. We'd never been separated since I got her. I had wanted to give her a puppy tranquilizer, but the vet cautioned me against it, saying animals didn't always do well at high altitude with drugs in their system.

"She may develop breathing problems and you won't be able to check on her," he'd said.

I tried to stay calm. As we said goodbye to Jerry and Sue-Ellen, the kids cried. Once we made it to the boarding gate, their hysteria evaporated. An adventure! They ran from seat to seat, bugging adults and children alike. I could only get them to sit down with the promise of pizza and sodas.

"Sodas?" Cherise arched a brow at me. The kids weren't allowed sodas at home.

"It's a special treat," I said.

They were so happy, that they were as good as gold the whole way to Toronto. They were adorable, actually. They watched movies, listened to music. Garnet danced in her seat to her favorite singer Rihanna, and then fell asleep tucked into her brother's arm. I took a photo with my cell phone to show Diego.

We arrived at Toronto Airport just after midnight. We'd had a stopover in Atlanta and the kids were exhausted. Diego was there to meet us as soon as we came out of customs. I almost didn't recognize him. I was bleary-eyed, and the haircut and clothing were a shock to my system. He looked good though. He reached for me and hugged and kissed me. I almost collapsed then. He smelled like Diego. He was real. He was alive. I was torn between the desire to beat the shit out of him and to undress him and lick every inch of his body.

"Asshole," I whispered in his ear.

He grinned, the bastard, then hugged the kids and Cherise.

He'd booked us into a couple of rooms at the Nu Hotel a mile away from the airport for the night, and in the morning, we'd fly to Montreal and then we'd have to drive to North Hatley.

"One room has two double beds, the other has one. I'm hoping Cherise will sleep with the kids so I can have some private time with you," he told me.

I hoped so, too. We all went off to collect Beauty. I was a little worried because she was shivering when I got her into the minivan Diego had rented. Being a pit bull, her coat was thin, and the cargo hold must have been chilly. Toronto was cool, and it had clearly rained, but once we let her out to pee on the sidewalk outside the hotel, she seemed much happier.

She greeted Diego with her typical mad rush of affection and then had to sniff every blade of grass she could find.

Diego had bought food for her, and she ate quickly, then drank almost a gallon of water once we hit the room. The kids wanted to sleep in our room, sharing a double bed. We didn't argue. We took the other.

Cherise had her room all to herself. "I'm going to take a bath," she announced. "I'm so happy!"

"We have to behave," Diego whispered to me after we tucked the kids into their bed. "Worst luck."

Yes, and no. I slept better than I had in weeks. It was the first time in a long, long time that I didn't dream of Garnet Beauty. I wished I had brought her tree with us. I would send for some seeds of a Garnet Beauty peach and plant one in North Hatley in her honor. I thought I would wake up constantly to check that Diego was there, but I didn't.

I slept the sleep of those who finally feel they are home. I wanted him so badly, it hurt. But I was grateful to be in his arms, and ecstatic to be here in Canada. At last.

Beauty left the confines of her comfy pile of blankets and plunked herself between us on the bed. *Thank God she doesn't snore.*

In the morning, we awoke, showered, and changed, and that was when I saw that Diego had removed his gang tattoo.

I touched the skin on his back.

"Did it hurt?"

"You got no idea," he said. We packed our things, walked Beauty, grabbed some breakfast, and headed back to the airport. The kids were happier than I'd ever seen them until Diego left us to return the van.

"He'll be back," I kept assuring them. I had a few qualms myself about my incredible, disappearing man. But he soon returned to us, and the kids hijacked him as we waited for our plane. I sat with Cherise, who professed both relief and disappointment over Maurice.

"I can't tell if it's killing me or making me stronger," she mused. "But I figure, I beat cancer. That makes him a piece of cake."

She was wonderful. I hugged her, aware of Diego's watchful gaze as the kids kept asking him a million questions about North Hatley and Canada. On the flight, they became increasingly excited. We flew lower on this craft than our international one, so they were able to pick out landmarks.

"Look! Snow! I could reach that with my tongue!" Henry shouted at one point, making other passengers laugh. When our one-hour flight was almost over, they glued their little faces to the windows of the plane to watch our descent.

We collected our dog and our suitcases, then Diego took us to the big SUV he'd left parked at the airport the day before.

About an hour and a half later, when we drove into North Hatley, everyone started to smile.

"It looks like home," Henry told me, his little cheeks pink with pleasure.

And it did. The air was crisp and fragrant.

"I smell pine trees," Garnet said, sniffing deeply. She looked so much like my sister in that moment it almost broke my heart. I held her to me. She hugged me back. My Garnet was here, in body, and in spirit. I wish I could have taken her away from her terrible life, but I knew she was here, enjoying every second of our new life.

Henry slipped his hand into mine. Even Beauty was quiet as we drove home, wedged in the back between me and the kids. Cherise sat up front, quietly filling Diego in on the details about his dad.

He looked pained when I caught his gaze in the rearview mirror. Whatever happened when we reached the town and the house, he'd found for us all, I needed and wanted him. We had to have sex. And soon.

When we arrived at the lake, the kids oohed and aahed.

Beauty wanted out, so we opened the door and let her run for a couple of minutes. She hopped in circles. I knew a big dump was coming.

"Eeew!" the kids shrieked. Of course, I was the one who had to clean up after her.

We got back into the SUV and arrived at the house. The kids couldn't wait to explore it.

"It's beautiful," Cherise said as we walked inside.

"Can you keep an eye on the children for us?" he asked her.

She smiled widely at him. "Of course. How about we make some lunch?"

That sounded good to us. Diego led me to the room that would be ours, and it felt right. From outside I could hear the sounds of a lake I'd never seen before and the rustle of trees, now my own.

Diego slowly undressed me. I waited for him to reach my pants zipper and I pushed him to the bed.

"It has good bounce," I muttered.

He grinned up at me. "Glad you like it." His eyes blazed with a raw hunger I hadn't seen for a long, long time. Could this really be it? Could we be together, no holds barred? No fear. No regrets. Was it really our time?

I gazed down at him, the full impact of everything we'd been through humbling me. Some people went through worse and didn't find love at the end of the fire.

"We have to find Cherise a man," I said.

"You're gonna talk about that now?" He reached up and pulled me to the bed. My cock was hard, and he palmed it, making appreciative sounds. He was hard inside the jeans he wore, and I couldn't wait to release him.

Diego was a willing 'undressee,' and removing his shirt, shoes, and socks were not a problem. But getting his pants down his thighs proved almost impossible.

I almost went berserk. I'd waited so long and wouldn't be denied this man a moment longer. He laughed as I tore at his clothing.

"I'm not going anywhere," he said, his voice thick with desire.

"So you say. I'm not taking any chances." I got his jeans over his hips, and his thick, engorged cock jutted against my chin. I sucked him into my mouth, and his ass flew off the bed. I knelt beside him, not letting go of him for a single second. He grabbed my hips and swung me over him, turning me so that I was facing away from him, my ass settling down right over his mouth.

He sucked and licked me in a frenzy.

This was actually a beautiful position because I could lean

down and suck him, too, but he kept twisting himself away from me. I finally understood. His cock was leaking every-where. He was afraid he'd come if I kept working on him. I didn't care. I was ready to explode myself.

I ignored his efforts to keep his cock away from my mouth, and I sucked his length in once more. He came so hard I saw stars as he fucked my throat with deep thrusts. I came, too, all over his chest. It was over so fast, neither of could speak for a moment. And then we grew hard again. Fast.

When he was ready to fuck again, he pushed me off his face and shoved me down to his cock, gasping for air. "Get me inside you," he rasped.

I slid down quickly and, soon, we were both working to get his raw, juicy cock inside me. It hurt so good. It had been so long since he'd been in me. He kept thrusting into me, and I bore down on him until at last he was completely submerged. We both moaned. Man, it was so great not to have to worry about being quiet or getting caught.

Then, "Uncle Colby?"

I almost screamed when my niece knocked at the door. Through the sexual haze in which we were both submerged, Diego and I spoke at once.

"Locked," we muttered to one another.

"Shhh," Cherise said outside. "They'll be out in a few minutes, sweetie."

"But I want him to come now," Garnet whined.

"You'll soon get your wish," I whispered. Diego laughed as I ground my body down on top of his. He reached up, grabbing my shoulders.

"Hot ass," he said. "I fucking missed you."

"Yeah." I panted. "I missed you, too."

He fucked me with abandon and reached around with one hand to jerk me off. I loved the way he moved inside me, the way he touched me. Just having him so close and so turned on made me giddy with joy. We came together, our bodies slick with sweat.

"That took the edge off," he said when I rolled off him and lay beside him.

"Speak for yourself, bitch. I just got started."

From somewhere, music played, and children laughed. Nothing mattered, though, but this man, and this moment.

"I'm all yours," he said, looking into my eyes, seeing the smoky lust mirrored there.

"Yeah, Diego." I took his face in my hands and kissed him. "I know."

YOU MAY ALSO ENJOY THE FOLLOWING FROM EXTASY BOOKS INC:

Haywire
A. J. Llewellyn and D. J. Manly
Release date

Excerpt

"Can we go on this, Daddy? Can we?"

The line wasn't long, but one of the amusement park officers standing nearby overheard their conversation.

"You should take the studio tour now," she advised. "You'll be able to go through the old Wisteria Lane set for Desperate Housewives. They're using it as the location for a new movie. If you wait, they'll be in production, and you'll miss seeing it."

"Cool!" Dex and Jack chimed in unison.

"What's Wisteria Lane?" their son wanted to know. He wasn't happy about the detour until they'd descended the ten thousand, or so it seemed, levels of moving stairs to get to the entrance for the studio tour. Nicky grumbled until he saw the attendant passing out 3D glasses for the ride.

"Oh yeah!" he shouted, excited again.

The line moved quickly, and their tram driver proved to be quite the comedian. On a video screen above them, Jimmy Fallon, the tour's official comedian, was playing guitar and cracking jokes. Nicky wore his 3D glasses even though they'd been instructed to wait. He was riveted by everything he saw.

Jack's heart swelled with love for his child. Twenty-five years ago, at the age of eight, Jack had come to the studio tour with his parents for the first time. He'd loved every second of it. Back in those days, there had been no rides. The tour was the entire thing. He would never forget Lucille Ball coming out of her dressing room to wave to the occupants of the tour tram. From that moment on, Jack had been in love with Hollywood movies and longed to be a part of it. Now he was, and he adored his work. Thanks to the magic of telecommuting, he could live in the place he wanted, yet do the job of his dreams.

As if on cue, they passed a slew of posters for Universal's upcoming fall release, the vampire movie, Banpaia.

"There's your campaign, sweetie," Dex said, snapping a pic of one of the posters.

It had been one of the biggest joys for Jack, creating a successful, award-winning promotion for a movie about gay vampires in Little Tokyo. He'd managed to snag a marketing bonanza with a limited edition, prerelease graphic novel and billboards all over town saying, Banpaia is Coming.

Jack felt warm and squishy inside, proud of his work. He kept his arm around his son as they ventured into Old Mexico and a simulated flash flood. Nicky, however, took it in stride.

"Way cool!" he shrieked, water splattering his 3D glasses. When the kid finally got to the 3D portion of the tour—the breathtaking and utterly astonishing battle between King Kong and the dinosaurs from Jurassic Park, Nicky went into orbit.

"I want to go back on it," he said as soon as the tour concluded. Dex was happy, too. He'd glimpsed Felicity Huffman, his favorite actress in the whole wide world, running past the bus tour, her hair in curlers. She'd waved to the crowd, and they waved right back.

"She's working on a new TV series, which is kinda hush-hush," the tour guide had said over the loudspeaker.

Nicky pulled at his fathers' hands. "Come on. We have to go on The Mummy. Then we can come back and take the tour again."

The line for The Mummy took thirty minutes. Dex left his family to queue, while he went to the locker room and stowed the backpack in one of the units. When he returned, he showed the park map to Jack and pointed out a special feature for the ride.

"Look, they've got this thing called Child Switch. We can take turns going on the ride with Nicky. They have a special holding area where one parent waits while the other one rides."

"Sounds good," Jack said. He'd hoped they could all ride together, but the attendant loading people onto the roller coaster said that they'd have a more comfortable ride with only two people in each set of seats.

Jack went first with Nicky, who loved it. He screamed and waved his arms in the air. He seemed fearless. The ride was over quickly. Jack traded places with Dex and stood in a freezing section to the left of the landing bay and waited for his family to return. He had the weirdest feeling . . . a pang of separation anxiety he couldn't explain.

I worry too much. I have to relax. I have to stop thinking something will happen to Nicky. Millions of people take this ride, and they don't fall out of the roller coaster. Dex loves Nicky. He'll protect him.

He stood and waited, watching out for his husband and son. A family came to stand beside him, exchanging with him the tight smiles strangers always did. And then a man and a child approached him.

"Daddy, that was sooooo cool!" The little boy stared up at him.

At first, Jack thought the kid was talking to the people beside him. Then he realized the child was talking to him. He stared at the little boy. A lump started forming in his throat. The kid was dressed exactly like Nicky.

The man who stood with his hands resting on the child's shoulders beamed at him. He was dressed exactly like Dex.

Except they weren't Dex and Nicky.

"Who are you?" Jack asked. This was freaky. How could they be dressed exactly like his husband and son?

"It's me," the man said. He looked exasperated. "It's me. Dex. Don't you recognize me?"

"What's wrong, Daddy?" the little boy asked, his round blue eyes staring up at Jack.

He wasn't Nicky. No. No. No.

Jack began to scream.

The little boy began to cry.

And Jack's world had just gone haywire . . .

ABOUT THE AUTHOR

A.J. Llewellyn is the author of almost three hundred published gay romance novels. A.J. lives in California, but dreams of living in Hawaii. Frequent trips to all the islands, bags of Kona coffee in the fridge and a healthy collection of Hawaiian records keep A.J. refueled.

A.J's passion for the islands led to writing a play about the last ruling monarch of Hawaii, Queen Lili'uokalani. A.J. has written a non-erotic novel about the overthrow of her kingdom written in diary form from her maid's point of view.

A.J. never lacks inspiration for male/male erotic romances and has to prise fingers from the computer keyboard to pursue other passions: collecting books on Hawaiiana, surfing and spending time with family, friends and animal companions.

D.J. Manly: I write not only for my own pleasure but for the pleasure of my readers. I can't remember a time in my life when I haven't written and told stories. When I'm not writing, I'm dreaming about writing, doing something wild and adventurous, or trying to make the world a better and more open-minded place to live in. I adore beautiful men, and I know I'm not alone in this! Eroticism between consenting adults, in all its many forms, is the icing on the cake of life!

D.J. has published well over two-hundred novels/novellas and is a well-seasoned writer.